Edmund Hodgson Yates

The Forlorn Hope
Vol. 3

ISBN/EAN: 9783337258191

Printed in Europe, USA, Canada, Australia, Japan

Cover: Foto ©Andreas Hilbeck / pixelio.de

More available books at **www.hansebooks.com**

THE FORLORN HOPE.

𝔄 𝔑𝔬𝔳𝔢𝔩.

BY

EDMUND YATES,

AUTHOR OF " RUNNING THE GAUNTLET," " KISSING THE ROD," ETC.

IN THREE VOLUMES.

VOL. III.

LONDON:

TINSLEY BROTHERS, 18 CATHERINE ST., STRAND.

1867.

LONDON :

ROBSON AND SON, GREAT NORTHERN PRINTING WORKS,

PANCRAS ROAD, N.W.

Edmund Hodgson Yates

The Forlorn Hope

Vol. 3

CONTENTS.

THE FORLORN HOPE.

CHAPTER I.

THE GULF FIXED.

FAINTED! a preposterous thing for a big strong man to do! Fainted, as though he had been a school-girl, or a delicate miss, or a romantic woman troubled with nerves. Mr. Walsingham did not understand it at all. He rang the bell, and told the servant to get some water and some brandy, and something—the right sort of thing; and he picked up Wilmot's head, which was gravitating towards the floor, and he bade him "Hold up, my good fellow!" and then he let his friend's head fall, and gazed at him with extreme bewilderment. He was unused to this kind of performance

was Mr. Walsingham, and felt himself eminently
helpless and ridiculous. When the water and the
brandy were brought, he administered a handful
of the former externally, and a wine-glassful of
the latter internally; and Wilmot revived, very
white and trembling and dazed and vacant-look-
ing. So soon as he could gather where he was,
and what had occurred, he made his apologies to
Mr. Walsingham, and begged he would add to the
kindness he had already shown by sending for a
cab, and by allowing him to borrow the newspaper
which he had been reading at the time of the
attack; it should be carefully returned that afternoon. Mr. Walsingham, who was the soul of
politeness, agreed to each of these requests; the
cab was fetched, and Wilmot, with many thanks
to his young friend, and with the packet for his
young friend's mother, his own passport, and the
Morning Post in his pocket, went away in it. Mr.
Walsingham, who regarded this little episode in
his monotonous life as quite an adventure, waxed
very eloquent upon the subject afterwards to his
friends, and made it his stock story for several

days. " Doosid awkward," he used to say, "to have a fellow, don't you know, who you don't know, don't you know, gone off into fits, and all that kind of thing! Here, too, of all places in the world! If he'd gone off in my rooms, you know, it wouldn't so much have mattered; but here, where old Blowhard"—for by this epithet Mr. Walsingham designated Sir Hercules Shandon, K.P., Her Britannic Majesty's Minister at the Court of Prussia—" where old Blowhard might have come in at any moment, don't you know, it might have been devilish unpleasant for a fellow. What he wanted with the *Post* I can't make out. I've looked through every column of it since he sent it back, but I can't find anything likely to upset a fellow like that. I thought at first he must have been sinking his fees in some city company that had bust-up, but there's no such thing in the paper; or that he'd read of some chap being poisoned in mistake, and that had come home to him, but there's nothing about that either. I can't make it out.—I say, Tollemache, do you see that Miss Kilsyth's married? Married to Caird, that good-looking fellow that always used to be there at Brook-street—tame cat in the house—and that used to—you know—Adalbert Villa, Omicron-road, eh? Sell for you, old boy; you were very hard hit in that quarter, weren't you, Tolly?"

So Chudleigh Wilmot went back to his hotel in the cab; and the friendly waiter, who had seen him depart so full of life and joyousness, had to help him up the steps, and thought within himself that the great English doctor would have to seek the assistance of other members of his craft. But no bodily illness had struck down Chudleigh Wilmot; he had not recovered his full strength, and the shock to his nerves had been a little too strong—that was all. So soon as he found himself alone, after refusing the friendly waiter's offer of sending for a physician, of getting him restoratives of a kind which came specially within the resources of the Hôtel de Russie, such as a roast chicken and a bottle of sparkling Moselle, and after dispensing with all further assistance or companionship, Wilmot locked the door of his room, and sat down at the table with the newspaper spread open before him. He read the paragraph again and again, with an odd sort of bewildering wonderment that it remained the same, and did not change before his eyes. No doubt about what it expressed—none. Madeleine Kilsyth, who had been worshipped by him for months past, and with whom as his companion he was looking forward to pass his future, was married to another man—that last fact was expressed in so many words. It was all over now, the hope and the fear and the longing; there was an end to it all. If he had only known this three months ago, what an agony of heart-sickness, of dull despair, of transient hope, of wearying feverish longing he had been spared! She was gone, then, so far as he was concerned—taken from him; the one star that had glimmered on his dark lonely path was quenched, and henceforward he was to stumble through life in darkness as best he might. That was a cruel trick of Fortune's, a wretched cruel trick, to keep him back in his pursuit, to throw obstacles of every kind in his way, but all the time to let him see his love at the end of the avenue, as he thought, beckoning to him to over-

come them all, to make his way to her, and carry
her off in spite of all opposition; then for all the
obstacles to melt away, for him to have naught to
do but gain the temple unopposed; and when he
succeeded in gaining it, for the doors to be open,
the shrine abandoned, the divinity gone!

Hard fate indeed! hard, hard fate! But
it was not to be. His dead wife had said it;
Henrietta Prendergast had said it: it was not to
be. For him no woman's love, no happy home,
no congenial spirit to share his thoughts, his
ambition, his success. He sighed as he thought
of this, with additional sadness as he remembered
that if Henrietta Prendergast's story were true,
all this had been his. Such a companion he had
had, had never appreciated, and had lost. He
had entertained an angel unawares, and he was
never to have the chance again. For him a
drear blank future—blank save when remorse
for the probable fate of the woman who had died
loving him, regret for the loss of the woman
whom he had loved, should goad him into new
scenes of fresh action. Madeleine married!

Was, then, his fancy that she, that Madeleine, during that interview in the drawing-room in Brook-street, had manifested an interest in him different from that which she had previously shown, a mere delusion? Had he been so far led away by his vanity as to mistake for something akin to his own feeling the mere gratitude which the young girl had felt towards her physician? Was she, indeed, " his grateful patient," and no more? Wilmot's heart sunk within him, and his cheeks burned, as this view of the subject presented itself to his mind. Had he, professing to be skilled in psychology, committed this egregious blunder? Had he, who was supposed to know what people really were when they had put off the mummeries which they played before the world, and when they had laid by their face-makings and their posturings and their society antics, and revealed to their physician perforce what no one else was allowed to see — had he been deceived in his character study of one who to him was a mere child? The very suddenness of the inspiration had led him to believe in its truth. Until that moment, just before that savage brother of hers had burst in upon them, he had acknowledged to himself the existence of his own passion indeed, but had struggled against it, fully believing it to be unreciprocated, fully believing in the mere gratitude and respect which—as it now seemed—were the sole feelings by which Madeleine had been animated. But surely that day, in her downcast eyes and in her fleeting blush, he had recognised——A new idea, which rushed through his mind like a flash of light, illumining his soul with a ray of hope. Had this been a forced marriage? Had she been compelled by her brother, her father, Lady Muriel—God knows who— to accept this alliance? Had it been carried out against her own free will? Had his absence from England been made the pretext for urging her on to it? Had that been shown to her as a sign of the mistake she had made in supposing that he, Wilmot, cared for her at all? He had never been so near the truth as now, and yet he scouted the notion more quickly than any of the others which he discussed within himself. Such a thing was impossible. The idea of a girl being forced to marry against her will, of her judgment being warped, and the truth perverted for the sake of warping that judgment, was incomprehensible to a man like Wilmot—man of the world in so many phases of his character, but of child-like simplicity in the others. He had heard of such things as the stock-in-trade of the novelist, but in real life they did not exist. Mammon-matches, forced marriages, diabolical torturings of fact—all these various combinations, neatly dovetailed together, filled the shelves of the circulating-library, but were laughed to scorn by all sensible persons when they professed to be accurate representations of what takes place in the every-day life of society.

Besides, if it were so, the mischief was done, and he was all-powerless to counteract it. The marriage had taken place; there was an end of it. It could be undone by no word or deed of his. The times were changed from the old days when a sharp sword and a swift steed could nullify the priest's blessing, and leave the brave gallant and

the unwilling bride to be "happy ever after."
He was no young Lochinvar, to swim streams
and scour countries, to dance but one measure,
drink one cup of wine, and bolt with the lady
on his saddle-croup. He was a sober, middle-
aged man, who must get back to England by the
mail-train and the packet-boat; and when he
got there—well, make his bow to the bride and
bridegroom, and congratulate them on the happy
event. It was all over. His turn in the wheel
of Fortune had arrived too late; the bequest
which his good old friend had secured to him,
had it come two months earlier, might have
insured his happiness for life: as it was, it left
him where it found him, so far as his great object in life, so far as Madeleine Kilsyth, was concerned.

Another long pause for reflection, a prolonged
pacing up and down the room, revolving all the
circumstances in his mind. Was his whole life
bound up in this young girl? did his whole
future so entirely hang upon her? Here was
he in his prime, with fame such as few men

ever attained to, with fortune newly accruing to
him—large fortune, leaving him his own master
to do as he liked, free, unfettered, with no ties
and no responsibilities; and was he to give up
this splendid position, or, not giving it up, to
forego its advantages, to let its gold turn into
withered leaves and its fruits into Dead-Sea
apples, because a girl, of whose existence he had
been ignorant twelve months before, preferred to
accept a husband of her choice, of her rank, of her
family connection, rather than await in maiden-
hood a declaration of his hitherto unspoken love?
He was pining under his solitude, the want of
being appreciated, the lack of someone to confide
in, to cherish, to educate, to love. Was his choice
so circumscribed by fate that there was only one
person in the world to fulfil all these require-
ments? Was it preordained that he must either
win Madeleine Kilsyth or pass the remainder of
his days helplessly, hopelessly celibate? Was his
heart so formed as to be capable of the reception
of this one individual and none other, to be im-
pressionable by her and her alone? His pride

revolted at the idea; and when a man's pride undertakes the task of combating his passion, the struggle is likely to be a severe one, and none can tell on which side the victory may lie.

He would test it, at all events, and test it at once. The kind old man now gone to his rest had hoped that the fortune which he had bequeathed might be of service to the son of his old friend "and to Mrs. Wilmot;" and why should it not, although Mrs. Wilmot might not be the person whom Mr. Foljambe had intended, nor, as Chudleigh had madly hoped on reading his benefactor's letter, Madeleine Kilsyth? He would go back to England at once; he would show these people that—even if they entertained the idea which had been so plainly set before him by Ronald Kilsyth—he was not the man to sink under an injury, however much he might suffer under an injustice. "Love flows like the Solway, but ebbs like its tide," so far he would say to them with Lochinvar; they should not imagine that he was going to pine away the remainder of his life miserably because Miss

Kilsyth had chosen to marry someone else. He had been a fool, a weak pliable fool, to make such a statement as he had done in that interview with Ronald Kilsyth. His cheeks tingled with shame as he remembered how he had confessed the passion which he had nurtured, and which he acknowledged beset him even at the time of speaking. And that cool, calculating young man, with his cursed priggish, pedantic airs, his lack of anything approaching enthusiasm, and his would-be frank manner, was doubtless at that moment grinning to himself at the successful result of his calm diplomacy. Chudleigh Wilmot stamped his foot on the floor and ground his teeth in the impotence of his rage.

Married to Ramsay Caird, eh? Ramsay Caird! Well, they had not made such a great catch after all! To hear them talk, to see the state they kept up at Kilsyth, to listen to or look at my Lady Muriel, one would have thought that an earl, with half England in estates at his back, was the lowest they would have stooped to for their daughter's husband. And now she was married to an untitled Scotchman, without money, and—well, if he remembered club-gossip aright, rather a loose fish. Had not Captain Kilsyth been a little too hurried in the clinching of the nail, in the completion of the bargain? As Mr. Foljambe's heir, he, Chudleigh Wilmot, would have been worth a dozen such men as Ramsay Caird; and as to the question of former intimacy, of acquaintance formed during his wife's life-time, the world would have forgotten that speedily enough.

He would go back to England at once, but when there he would show them he was not the kind of man which, from Ronald Kilsyth's behaviour, that family apparently imagined him. Still the Border song rang in his head—

"There were maidens in Scotland more lovely by far
Would gladly be bride to the young Lochinvar."

Not more lovely, and probably never to be anything like so dear to him; but there were other maidens in England besides Madeleine Kilsyth. And why should the remainder of his life be to him utterly desolate because this girl either

did not love him, or, loving him, was weak enough
to yield to the interference of others? Was he
to pine in solitude, to renounce all the pleasures
of wifely companionship, to remain, as he had
hitherto been, self-contained and solitary, because
he had placed his affections unworthily, and they
had not been understood, or cast aside? No;
he had existed, he had vegetated long enough;
henceforward he would live. · Wealth and fame
were his; he was not yet too old to inspire
affection or to requite it; by his old friend's death
he had obtained an additional claim upon society,
which even previously was willing enough to
welcome him; he should have the *entrée* almost
where he chose, and he would avail himself of
the privilege. So thus it stood. Chudleigh Wilmot left London broken-hearted at having to give
up his love, and full of remorse for a crime, not
of his commission indeed, but which he imagined
had arisen out of his own egotism and selfish
preoccupation. He was about to start on his
return, with stung sensibility and wounded pride
—feelings which rendered him hostile rather

than pitying towards the woman to whom he
had imagined himself sentimentally attached, and
which had completely obliterated and driven into
oblivion all symptoms of his remorse.

He wrote a hurried line to Messrs. Lambert
and Lee, informing them of his satisfaction with
their proceedings hitherto, and notifying his immediate return; and he told the friendly waiter
that he should start by that night's mail, and get
as far as Hanover. But this the friendly waiter
would not hear of. The Herr Doctor must know
perfectly well—for had not he, the friendly waiter,
heard the German doctors speak of the English
doctor's learning?—that he was in no condition
to travel that night. If he, the friendly waiter,
might in his turn prescribe for the English doctor, he should say, " Wait here to-night; dine,
not at the *table d'hôte*, where there is hurry and
confusion, but in the smaller *speise-saal*, where
you usually breakfast; and the cook shall be instructed to send up to you of his very best; and
the Herr Oberkellner, a great man, but to be come
over by tact, and specially kind in cases of illness,

shall be persuaded to go to the cellar and fetch you Johannisberg—not that Zeltinger or Marco-brünner, which, under the name of Johannisberg, they sell to you in England, but real Johannisberg, of Prince Metternich's own vintage—pfa!'" and the friendly waiter kissed his own fingers, and then tossed them into the air as a loving tribute to the excellence of the costly drink.

So Wilmot, knowing that there was truth in all the man had said; feeling that he was not strong, and that what little strength he had had gone out of him under the ordeal of the morning at the Embassy, gave way, and consented to remain that night. But the next morning he started on his journey, and on the evening of the third day he arrived in London. He drove straight to his house in Charles-street, and saw at once by the expression of his servant's face that the news of his inheritance had preceded him. There was a struggle between solemnity and mirth on the man's countenance that betrayed him at once. The man said he expected his master back, was not in the least surprised at his

coming; indeed most people seemed to have expected him before. What did he mean? O, nothing—nothing; only there had been an uncom-
mon number of callers within the last few days.
"Not merely the reg'lars," the man added; "them
of course; but there have been many people as we
have not seen here these two years past a rat-tat-
tin', and leavin' reg'lar packs of cards, with their
kind regards, and to know how you were, sir."
The cards were brought, and Wilmot looked
through them. The man was right; scores of his
old acquaintance, whom he had not seen or heard
of for years, were there represented; people whom
he had only known professionally, and who had
never been near him since he wrote their last
prescription and took their last fee months before,
had sought him out again. To what could this
be accredited? Either to the earnest desire of
all who knew him to console him in the affliction
of having lost his friend, or to the information
sown broadcast by that diligent contributor to the
Illustrated News, who had given exact particulars
of the will of the late John Foljambe, Esq., ban-

ker, of Lombard-street and Portland-place. But there was no card from any member of the Kilsyth family in the collection. Wilmot searched eagerly for one, but there was none there.

He had a hurried meal—hurried, not because he had anything to do, and wanted to get through with it, but because he had no appetite, and what was placed before him was tasteless and untempting—and sat himself down in his old writing-chair in his consulting-room to ponder over his past and his future. He should leave that house ; he must. Though Mr. Foljambe had made no binding requirement, the expression of his wish was enough. Wilmot must leave that house, and obey his benefactor's behests by taking up his residence in Portland-place. He had never thought much of it before, but now he felt that he loved the place in which so much of his life had been passed, and felt very loth to leave it. He recollected when he had first moved into it, when his practice began to increase and his name began to be known. He remembered how his friends had said that it was necessary he should take up his position in a good West-end street, and how alarmed he was, when the lease was signed and the furniture— rather scanty and very poor, but made to look its best by Mabel's disposition and taste — had been moved in, lest he should be unable to pay the heavy rent. He recollected perfectly the first few patients who had come to see him there : some sent by old Foljambe, some droppers-in from the adjacent military club, allured by the bright door-plate; old gentlemen wishing to be young again, and young gentlemen in constitution rather more worn and debilitated than the oldest of the veterans. He remembered his delight when the first great person ever sent for him; how he had treasured the note requesting his visit; how he had gone to his club and slily looked up the family in the Peerage ; and how when he first stood before Lady Hernshaw, and listened to her account of her infant's feverish symptoms, he could, if he had been required, have gone through an examination in the origin and progress of the Hawke family, with the names of all the sons and daughters extant, and come out triumphantly. His well-loved books were ranged in due order on the walls round him; on the table before him stood the lamp by whose light he had gathered and reproduced that learning which had gained him his fame and his position. In that house all his early struggles had been gone through; he remembered the first dinner-parties which had been given under Mabel's superintendence, her diffidence and fright, his nervousness and anxiety. And now that was all of the past; Mabel had vanished for ever and aye; and soon the old house and its belongings, its associations and traditions, would know him no more. What had he gained during those few years? Fame, position, men's good word, the envy of his brother-professionals, and, recently, wealth. What had he lost? Youth, spirit, energy, the at one time all-sufficing love of study and progress in his science, content; and, latterly, the day-spring of a new existence, the hope of a new world which had opened so fairly and so promisingly before him. The balance was on the *per-contra* side, after all.

The fashionable journals found out his return

(how, his servant of all men alone knew), and proclaimed it to the world at large. The world at
large, consisting of the subscribers to the said
fashionable journals, acknowledged the information, and the influx of cards was redoubled.
Some of these performers of the card-trick lingered at the door, and entered into conversation
with the presiding genius in black to whom their
credentials were delivered. Whether the doctor
were well, whether he intended continuing the
practice of his profession, whether the rumour
that he intended giving up that house and re-
moving to Portland-place had any substantial
foundation; whether it were true that he, the presiding genius, was about to have a new mistress, a
lady from abroad—for some even went so far as
to make that inquiry—all these different points
were put, haughtily, confidentially, jocosely, to the
presiding genius of the street-door, and all were
answered by him as best he thought fit. Only one
of the queries, the last, had any influence on that
great man. He fenced with it in public with all
the coolness and the dexterity of an Angelo, but

in private, in the sacred confidence of the pantry engendered by the supper-beer, he was heard to declare that "the guv'nor knew better than that; or that if he didn't, and thought to introduce furreners, with their scruin' ways, to sit at the 'ead of his table and give horders to them, he'd have to suit himself, and the sooner he knew that the better.".

Some of the callers on seeking admittance were admitted—among them Dr. Whittaker. Perhaps amongst the large circle of Wilmot's acquaintances calling themselves Wilmot's friends, that eminent practitioner was the only one who had a direct and palpable feeling of annoyance at Wilmot's return.

Dr. Whittaker's originally good practice had been considerably amplified by the patients who, under Wilmot's advice, had yielded themselves up to Dr. Whittaker's direction during Wilmot's absence, and the substitute naturally looked with alarm upon the reappearance of the great original. So Dr. Whittaker presented himself at an early date in Charles-street, and being admitted, had a long and, on his side at least, an earnest talk with his friend. After the state and condition of various of the leading patients had been discussed between them, Whittaker began to touch upon more dangerous, and to him more interesting, ground, and said, with an attempt at jocosity,—and Whittaker was a ponderous man, in whom humour was as natural and as easy as it might have been in Sir Isaac Newton,—

"And now that I have given account of my stewardship, I suppose my business is ended, and all I have to do is to return my trust into the hands of him from whom I received it."

He said this with a smile and a smirk, but with an anxious look in his eyes notwithstanding.

"I don't clearly understand you," said Wilmot. "If you mean to ask me whether I intend to take up my practice again, my answer is clear and distinct—No. If you wish to inquire whether those patients whom you have been attending in my absence will continue to send for you, I am in no position to say. All I can say is, that if they send for me, I shall let them know that I have retired from the profession, and that you are taking my place."

Dr. Whittaker was in ecstasies. "Of course that is all I could expect," he replied; "and I flatter myself that—hum! ha! well, a man does not boast of his own proceedings—ha! Well then, and so what the little birds whispered *is* true, eh?"

"I—I beg your pardon," said Wilmot absently—"the—the little birds—"

"Cautious!" murmured Dr. Whittaker in his blandest tone—that tone which had such an influence with female patients—"we are quite right to be cautious; but between friends one may refer to the little birds which have whispered," he continued with surprising unction, "that a certain friend of ours, whom the world delights to honour, has succeeded to wealth and station, and is about to exchange that struggle in which the—the, if I may so express it—the *pulverem Olympicum* is gathered, for a soft easy seat in the balcony, whence he can look on at the contention with a smiling *conjux* by his side."

" Little birds have peculiar information, Whittaker, if they have been so communicative as all that," said Wilmot with a rather dreary smile; " they know more than I do, at all events."

" Ha, ha! my dear friend," said Whittaker, in a gushing transport of delight at the thought of his own good fortune; " we are deep, very deep; but we must allow a little insight into human affairs to others. Why did we fly from the world, dear Bessy, to thee? as the poet Moore, or Milton —I forget which—has it. Why did we give up our practice, and hurry off so suddenly to foreign parts, hum?" Dr. Whittaker gave this last " hum" in his softest and most seductive tones, such tones as had never failed with a patient. But perhaps because Wilmot was not a patient, and was indeed versed in the behind-scenes mechanism of the profession, it had no effect on him, and he merely said: " Not for the reason you name. Indeed, you never were further out in any surmise."

" Is that really so?" said Whittaker blandly. " Well, well, you surprise me! It is only a fort- night since that I was discussing the subject at

a house where you seem often spoken of, and I
said I fully believed the report to be true."

"And where was that, pray?" asked Wilmot,
more for the sake of something to say than for
any real interest he took in the matter.

"Ah, by the way, you remind me! I intended to speak to you about that case before you
left. The young lady whom you attended in Scotland—where you were when poor Mrs. Wilmot
died, you know—"

"In Scotland — where I was when — good
God! what do you mean?"

"Miss Kilsyth, you know. Well, you left
her in charge of poor old Rowe as a special case,
didn't you? Yes, I thought so. Well, the poor
old gentleman got a frightful attack of bronchitis,
and was compelled to go back to Torquay—don't
think he'll last a month, poor old fellow!—and
before he went, he asked me to look after Miss
Kilsyth. Thought she had phthisis—all nonsense,
old-fashioned nonsense; merely congestion, I'm sure.
I've seen her half-a-dozen times; and about a fortnight ago—yes, just before her intended marriage

was announced—she's married since, you know—
we were talking about you, and I mentioned this
rumour, and—and we had a good laugh over your
enthusiasm."

" It is a pity, Dr. Whittaker," said Wilmot,
quivering with suppressed rage, " it is a pity; and
it is not the first time that it has been remarked,
both professionally and socially, that you offer
opinions and volunteer information on subjects of
which you are profoundly ignorant. Good-morn-
ing !"

Just before the announcement of her intended
marriage ! Had the vile nonsense talked by that
idiot Whittaker had any influence in inducing her
to take that step ? He thought of that a hundred
times, coming at last to the conclusion—what did
it matter now ? The irrevocable step was taken.
Ah, for him it was not to be ! His dead wife had
said so—Henrietta Prendergast had said so. It
was not to be !

What was to be was soon carried out accord-

ing to his old friend's expressed wish. Wilmot
removed from Charles-street to Portland-place,
and materially changed his manner of life. All
his old patients flocked round him directly his return was announced; but, as he had promised
Whittaker, he let it be understood that he had entirely retired from practice. He even declined to
attend consultations, alleging as an excuse that his
health was delicate, and that for some time at least
he required absolute repose. He had determined
to take as much enjoyment out of life as he could
find in it; and that, truth to tell, was little enough.
The growth and development of his love for Madeleine Kilsyth had lessened his thirst for knowledge and his desire for fame; and when the
fierce flames of that love had burned out, there
was still enough fire in the ashes to wither up
and destroy any other passion that might seek to
occupy his heart. He tried to find relief for the
dead weariness of spirit, the blank desolation always upon him, in society. He gathered around
him brilliant men of all classes; and " Wilmot's
dinners" were soon spoken of as among the plea-

santest bachelor *réunions* in London. He dined
out at clubs, he joined men's dinner-parties; but
he resolutely declined to enter into ladies' society.
The resolution which he had formed at the Berlin
hotel of proving to the Kilsyth people that there
were families equal to theirs into which he could
be received, and girls equal to Madeleine who
were willing to marry him, never was brought to
the test. Many ladies no doubt asked their husbands about Wilmot; but from the answers they
received they regarded him as never likely to
marry again; and save from hearsay report, they
had no opportunity of evidence.

He went about constantly, rode on horseback
a great deal, visited theatres, and sat with a melan-
choly face at nearly all the public exhibitions. The
few persons who had sufficient interest in him to
discuss the reason for this change attributed it to
the impossibility of his ever recovering the shock
of his wife's sudden death; and he was quoted
perpetually before many husbands, who sincerely
wished they had the opportunity of showing how
they would conduct themselves under similar cir-

cumstances. So his life passed on, monotonous, blank, aimless, for about three weeks after his installation in Portland-place; when one evening returning from a long ride round the western suburbs, as he turned his horse through the Albert-gate, he came full upon a carriage containing Lady Muriel and Madeleine. They were so close, that it was impossible to avoid a recognition. Wilmot raised his hat mechanically, Lady Muriel gave him a chilling bow, and then turned rapidly to her companion. Madeleine turned dead-white, and sank back as though she would have fainted; but Lady Muriel's look recalled her, and she recovered herself in time to bow. Then they were gone. Not much hope in that, Chudleigh Wilmot! Not much chance of bridging that gulf which is fixed between you!

CHAPTER II.

MRS. PRENDERGAST had heard of Chudleigh Wilmot's accession to fortune before the news had reached that more than ever "rising" man. Though she was not among Mr. Foljambe's intimates, and though that sprightly old gentleman found less favour in her eyes than in those of most of his acquaintance, she knew when his illness commenced, when it had assumed a dangerous form ; and she was one of the earliest outsiders to learn its fatal and rapid termination. She was indebted for all this information to Dr. Whittaker, whom she had assiduously cultivated, and who was very fond of talking of all and everything that nearly or remotely concerned Wilmot. The little professional jealousy which had sometimes interfered with Dr. Whittaker's genuine and ge-

nerally irrepressible admiration of the genius and
the success of his *confrère* and superior had given
way to the influence of the superior's loftiness and
liberality of mind ; and with Dr. Whittaker also
there was, as old Mr. Foljambe had said, on an
occasion destined to affect many destinies, "nothing like Wilmot."

Dr. Whittaker was not aware that Mrs. Prendergast valued his visits chiefly because they af-
forded her an opportunity, which otherwise she
could not have enjoyed, of hearing of Wilmot.
She had too much tact to permit him to make
any such mortifying discovery, and he had too
much vanity to permit him to suspect the
fact, except under extreme provocation. So Mrs.
Prendergast accounted his visits as among her
most agreeable glimpses of society ; and he regarded her as one of the most sensible and un-
affected women of his acquaintance. Thus, when
Dr. Whittaker's attendance on Mr. Foljambe came
to a close with the sprightly and *débonnaire* old
gentleman's life, he brought the news to his friend
in Cadogan-place, and they lamented together ·

Wilmot's untimely absence.   But Dr. Whittaker
had previously conveyed to Mrs. Prendergast information of another sort, which had largely in-
fluenced the feelings with which she heard of Mr.
Foljambe's death.

It was the same welcome messenger who had
brought her the tidings of Madeleine Kilsyth's
marriage; and never had he been more welcome.
She had steadily persevered in denying to herself
that the young Scotch girl could possibly count
for anything, one way or another, in the matter
in which she was so vividly interested; but she
had not succeeded in feeling such complete conviction on the point as to render her indifferent to
any occurrence which effectually disposed of that
young lady before Wilmot's return.   That he
should have come back to London, to all the former prestige of his talent and success, with the
new and brilliant addition that he had acquired
the whole of Mr. Foljambe's large fortune, to find
Madeleine Kilsyth unmarried, and to be brought
upon an equality with her by the agency of his
wealth,—this would not have appeared to Hen-

rietta by any means desirable. The obstacles which the social pride of her relations might have opposed to a *penchant* for Wilmot on the part of Miss Kilsyth—and Mrs. Prendergast had always felt instinctively that such a *penchant*, if it did not actually exist, would arise with opportunity— would be considerably modified, if not altogether removed, by Wilmot's becoming a rich man by other than professional means. Altogether there were many new sources of danger to her project, which did not relax in its intensity and fixedness by time, silence, or leisure for consideration, in the possibility of Madeleine Kilsyth's being again brought within Wilmot's reach, which presented themselves very unpleasantly to the clear perception of Mrs. Prendergast.

"And so you had not heard of Miss Kilsyth's intended marriage at all, knew nothing of it until after the event?" said Dr. Whittaker, after he had imparted the intelligence to Mrs. Prendergast. To him it was merely an item in the gossiping news of the day; nor had he any suspicion that it was more to his hearer.

"No; I had not heard a word of it. And I wonder I had not, for I have seen Miss Charlton several times; and I know Mrs. M'Diarmid has been at their house frequently. She must have known all about it, and I can't fancy her knowing anything and not talking about it."

"No," said Dr. Whittaker. "Reserve is not her *forte*, good old lady. But they say—the omnipresent, omniscient, and indefinable *they*—that Miss Kilsyth expressly stipulated that the engagement was to be kept a profound secret. She is troubled, I understand, with rather more delicacy and modesty than most young ladies at present; and she disliked the pointing and talking, the giggling and speculation which attend the appearance of an engaged young lady in what is politely called 'high life' on such occasions."

"The engagement was not a long one, I suppose?" said Henrietta.

"Only a few weeks, I understand. They say Lady Muriel Kilsyth was rather anxious to get her step-daughter off her hands—"

"And into those of her not particularly rich

cousin, I fancy," said Henrietta. Dr. Whittaker laughed.

" I daresay I shall hear a great deal about it at the Charltons'," she continued; " I am going to dine there to-morrow. I know Mrs. M'Diarmid will be there, and she will have plenty to tell, no doubt. I shall hear much more about the wedding than I shall care for."

Mrs. Prendergast dined at Mrs. Charlton's on the following day, and she did hear a great deal about the wedding, which Mrs. M'Diarmid was of opinion had not been quite worthy of the occasion either in style or in publicity, and whereat she could not say Madeleine had conducted herself altogether to her satisfaction. Not that she had been too emotional, or in the least bold in her manner, but she had taken it all so very quietly.

" I assure you it was quite unnatural, in my opinion," said the old lady, with a homely heartiness of manner calculated to convert other people to her opinion too. " Madeleine was as quiet and as unconcerned as if it was somebody else's wedding, and not her own. She positively seemed to think more of little Maud's dress and appearance than of her own, and she was as friendly as possible with Mr. Caird."

"Friendly with Mr. Caird, Mrs. M'Diarmid!" said Henrietta. "Why should you be surprised at that? Why should she not be friendly with him?"

"Well, I'm sure I don't know, my dear," answered Mrs. M'Diarmid, who called everyone 'my dear;' "it did seem odd to me somehow—there, I can't explain it; and I daresay I'm an old fool—very likely; but they did seem more like friends to me, that is, Madeleine did, than lovers—that's the truth."

Miss Charlton remarked to Mrs. Prendergast, with a sentimental sigh, that she perfectly understood Mrs. M'Diarmid,—that Miss Kilsyth's manner had had too little of the solemnity and exaltation of such a serious and important event. "At such a moment, Henrietta," said the young lady, raising her fine eyes towards the ceiling, "earth and its restraints should fade, and the spirit be devoted to the heavenly temple, which is the true scene of the marriage."

"All I can say, then," said Mrs. M'Diarmid, by no means touched by the high-flown interpretation placed upon her remarks, "is, that if anyone can be reminded of a heavenly temple by St. George's, Hanover-square, they must have a lively imagination; for a duller and heavier earthly one I never was in in my life."

"I suppose the wedding-party was numerous?" said Mrs. Charlton, who never could endure anything like a verbal passage-at-arms; and who was moreover occasionally beset by a misgiving that her daughter was rather silly.

"Not what the Kilsyths would consider large, my dear; only their immediate connections and a few very intimate friends. Miss Kilsyth would have it so; and indeed the whole thing was got up in a hurry. It was announced in the *Morning Post* on Monday, and the marriage came off on Wednesday."

"I suppose the bride had some splendid presents?" said Miss Charlton, whose curiosity was agreeably irrepressible.

"O yes, my dear, lots. Some beautiful and

expensive ; some ugly and more expensive ; several cheap and pretty; and a great many which could not possibly be of use to any rational being. You know Mr. Foljambe, don't you, Mrs. Prendergast ?"

" Yes," said Henrietta; "I know him slightly."

" He is an old friend of Kilsyth's; poor man, he's very ill indeed—could not come to the wedding because he was ill then, and he is much worse since; he gave Madeleine the handsomest present of the lot—a beautiful set of pearls, and he sent her such a nice, kind, old-fashioned letter with them. He is a real old dear, though I always feel a little afraid of him somehow."

" Is Mr. Foljambe really very ill ?" said Mrs. Charlton.

" I am sorry to say he is," said Henrietta ; " I saw Dr. Whittaker to-day, and he gave a very bad account of him."

" Dr. Whittaker ?" said Mrs. Charlton inquiringly. " I don't know him; I—"

" No," interrupted Henrietta with a smile; "he is not yet famous; he is only just beginning

to be a rising man. He is a great friend of
Dr. Wilmot's, who, when he went abroad, placed
several of his principal patients in his hands."

As Henrietta mentioned Wilmot's name, she
glanced keenly at Mrs. M'Diarmid, and perceived
at once that the mention of him produced an effect
on the old lady of no pleasing kind. Her face
became overcast in a moment.

"I hope Miss Kilsyth's—I beg her pardon,
Mrs. Caird's health is sufficiently restored to make
any such provision in her case unnecessary," said
Henrietta to Mrs. M'Diarmid in her best manner;
which was a very good manner indeed.

"Yes, yes," the old lady said absently; then
recovering herself, she continued, "Madeleine has
been much better latterly; but Sir Saville Rowe
has been looking after her. Dr. Wilmot recom-
mended her specially to his care."

The conversation then turned on other matters,
and did not again revert to the Kilsyths; but Mrs.
Prendergast carried away with her from the sub-
stance of what had passed two convictions.

The first, that Wilmot had entertained suffi-

cient feeling of some kind for Madeleine Kilsyth
to render him averse to bringing her into contact
with the man who attended his wife's death-bed,
and who might therefore have been inconveniently
communicative, or even suspicious.   •

The second, that there was some painful impression or association in the kind, honest, and
simple mind of Mrs. M'Diarmid connected with
Dr. Wilmot and Madeleine Kilsyth.

On that evening Mrs. Prendergast settled the
point, in consultation with herself, that Madeleine's marriage was an important advantage
gained. How important, or precisely why, she
had no means of ascertaining, but she felt that it
was so ; and she experienced a comfortable feeling,
compounded of hope and content, at the occurrence.

A week later Dr. Whittaker called on Henrietta and communicated to her the intelligence of
Mr. Foljambe's death ; and in a few days later the
accession of Wilmot to his faithful old friend's
large fortune was made known to her in the same
way.

And now Henrietta felt the full importance of
the removal of Madeleine Kilsyth from Wilmot's
path. He would return to London of course—
perhaps to abandon his professional pursuits,
though that she thought an unlikely step on
his part. His sphere of life would, however, certainly be changed; and the best chance for the
success of her project would consist in her being
able to induce him to form habits of intimacy and
companionship with her before the increased de-
mands of society upon him should whirl him away
out of her reach. Even supposing, which she—
though more capable than most women of taking
a contingency which she disliked into sensible and
serious consideration — did not think likely, that
Dr. Wilmot would contemplate a second marriage,
and that marriage purely of affection, he would
certainly return to London heart-whole. If Madeleine Kilsyth had indeed possessed for him attrac-
tion which he could not disavow to himself, nor
avow to the world, so much the better now as
things had turned out. Madeleine would have
held his fancy captive until such time as fate had

set between them a second inviolable barrier; and
this new and keen disappointment, even supposing
he had never distinctly formulated his hope, would
have turned his heart, and brought him back
irresistibly to the realities of life.

Thus, knowing nothing of the actual circumstances of the case; unaware of the twofold shock
which Chudleigh Wilmot had received by the
events which she calmly regarded as equally
fortunate; unconscious of the storm of passion,
rage, grief, and helplessness in which Wilmot was
wrapped and tossed, even while she was quietly
discussing the matter with herself, Henrietta
Prendergast arranged the present before her
eyes, and questioned the future in her thoughts.
But had she known all of which she was ignorant—had she been able to see Chudleigh Wilmot
as he really was, while she was thus thinking of
him, the revelation would hardly have changed
the current of her thoughts, though it might have
robbed her of much of her composure. In that
case she would have reflected that she had but
mistaken the quality and the depth of his feel-

ings, that circumstances remained unchanged. Wilmot had been passionately in love with Madeleine Kilsyth; but he was now none the less certainly, irrevocably, and eternally separated from her.

Thus, the facts which she knew, the facts which she guessed, and the facts which were effectually concealed from her, all bore encouragingly upon the projects of Henrietta Prendergast. It is only just to acknowledge that the increase to his wealth did not intensify or sharpen Mrs. Prendergast's wish to marry Wilmot; indeed it rather depressed her. She felt that it might create new obstacles as strong as those which fate had removed; she would have preferred his being in his former position. "If I could have won him as he was," she thought, "and then this fortune had come, that would have been better. However, ever so poor he would have been a man worth winning; it makes no difference in that respect his being ever so rich."

After all, this appreciation, calm and passionless, yet just, clear-sighted, and true, was not a gift to be despised by a sensible man, who had had the gilding pretty nearly taken off the gingerbread of his life, but it was not likely to be valued as it deserved by a man pining desperately for the impossible love of a brilliant young beauty like Madeleine Kilsyth.

One immediate purpose which Henrietta set strongly before her was to see Wilmot as soon as possible after his return, of the time of which event she would be duly informed by Dr. Whittaker. She had had no communication with him since the puzzling interview which had preceded his departure; he had neither written nor gone to take leave of her; but this omission, which would have been extremely discouraging to a less keen-sighted woman, was not discouraging to Henrietta. She knew that, as far as she was concerned, it meant simply nothing. Wilmot was deeply distressed and preoccupied; that was the cause of it. She also knew that at present, in his life, *she* meant nothing, and she was satisfied, so that the future should afford her a fair opportunity of coming to mean much. But she must attain and begin to profit by that opportunity as soon as possible—she must endeavour to anticipate other impressions; and for this purpose she resolved to seek an interview with him immediately on his return.

"I will write to him at once," she said to herself. "He has no reason to wish to avoid me; and if he had, he would conquer it at an appeal made in the name of poor Mabel."

And this strange yet matter-of-fact woman paused in the busy current of her thoughts and plans to bestow affectionate remembrance and true regret on her dead friend! Henrietta Prendergast was neither inconsistent nor insincere.

*   *   *   *   *

"I hope you did not think me intrusive in asking you to call on me so soon," said Henrietta to Chudleigh Wilmot, when he had duly presented himself in answer to a note from her, which she had written on the day Dr. Whittaker had told her Wilmot had returned to London.

"You have seen him, of course?" she had asked Dr. Whittaker.—"Yes, I have seen him.

He looks extremely ill—wretchedly ill, in fact. As unlike a man who has just come in for a tremendous stroke of luck as any man I ever saw. I fancy he was more cut up about his wife's death than either you or I gave him credit for—eh, Mrs. Prendergast?"

And now, holding Wilmot's hand in hers, and looking into his sunken eyes, marking his sallow cheek, the rigidity of the expression of his face, the thinness of his hand, she thought that Dr. Whittaker's first impressions were correct. He did look ill, wretchedly ill. He did indeed look little like a favourite of fortune.

He assured her, very kindly, that her note had only forestalled his intention of calling upon her immediately, and apologised for his former omission.

" I ought to have come to say good-bye," he said; " but I could not indeed. I made no adieux possible to be avoided."

" And have you benefited by your absence ? Have you gained health and spirits to enjoy the good fortune which has befallen you ?"

She asked him these questions in a tone of more than conventional kindness; but her face told him she read the answer in his.

"I am quite well," he said quickly; "but perhaps I don't enjoy my good fortune very much. I am alone in the world, Mrs. Prendergast; and my fortune has been gained by the loss of the best friend I ever had in it."

"Yes," she said thoughtfully, "that is very true. Poor Mr. Foljambe! He missed you very much; but," she added, for she saw the painful expression of self-reproach which she had noticed in their first interview after Mabel's death settle down upon his face, "you must not grieve about that. He expressed the utmost confidence in Dr. Whittaker."

"I know—I know," said Wilmot. "Still I wish—however, that is but one of many far heavier griefs. I did not come to talk about my troubles," he said with a faint smile. "You had something to say to me—what is it? Not only to congratulate me on being a rich man now that it is too late, I am sure."

"It is not altogether too late, I think," said Henrietta in a low impressive voice; "and I wanted to speak to you of something connected alike with your grief and your fortune."

"Indeed!" said Wilmot in a tone of anxious surprise.

"Yes," said Henrietta; "I did not know how long or how short a time you might be within my reach; and so I determined to lose no time in endeavouring to gain your assent to a wish of poor Mabel's."

The conscious blood rushed into Wilmot's face. This, then, was the double connection of his present visit with his grief and his fortune. And he had not been thinking of Mabel! His dead wife's friend believed him indifferent to the wealth that had come too late to be shared by her; and except for the first sudden remembrance which the sight of Henrietta had produced, he had not thought of his dead wife at all. He thought of her now with keen remorse—keener because it had not occurred to him to think of her before, in connection with his wealth. Yes, the life which had had so dark

an ending might have been very bright and pro-
sperous now, with all this useless money to gild it.
He shrunk from Mrs. Prendergast's steady eyes
with all the shame and uneasiness of a candid
nature when given credit for motives or deeds
superior to the truth. No vision of the dead face
he had seen, awfully white and still, in his little
loved home, had arisen to blot out the prospect of
a future rich in all that wealth can give, to teach
him how infinitely little is that all, how poor that
richness! But he carried about for ever between
him and the sunshine a vision of a fair girlish
face, with pleading innocent blue eyes, with golden
hair and faintly flushing cheeks, with sweet sensitive lips, and over all a look which he knew well
and interpreted only too accurately. And that
face, it did not lie in a coffin indeed, but as far,
as hopelessly away from him—it lay on another
man's breast. This was his grief; the other—well,
the other was his shield from suspicion, from ob-
servation, his defence. He seized upon it, feeling
unutterably the degradation of the evasion, and
answered :

" I will be more than grateful, Mrs. Prendergast, if you can show me any way in which I can
fulfil any wish of hers. If there is anything within
the power of any effort of mine, let me know it.'"

Then Henrietta, in her turn, putting the dead
woman forward as a pretext, began to discuss with
Wilmot the provisions of a certain charitable in-
stitution, to which she knew it had been Mrs. Wilmot's wish to contribute, but which she had not
felt entitled by her means to assist. Wilmot ac-
ceded to all her suggestions with the utmost readi-
ness, besought her to tax her memory for any
other resource for doing honour to Mabel's memory, and prolonged his visit considerably beyond
Henrietta's expectation. In her softened manner
there was now no reproach, and her sense and
calmness refreshed his jaded spirits. It was a relief to him to be in the company of a woman who
did not expect him to be anything but sorrowful,
and who yet had no suspicion of the cause and
origin of his sorrow. So thought Wilmot, as he
left Henrietta, having asked her permission to call
on her again speedily.

And at the same moment Henrietta was thinking—

"He knows something of the torture of love
unrequited and in vain now. It won't last, of
course; but for the present, if she could only know
it, poor Mabel is avenged!"

CHAPTER III.

Mr. and Mrs. Ramsay Caird lived, it is needless to say, in a fashionable quarter of the town. They could not have lived in any other. Their lot being essentially cast among fashionable people, it was necessary for them to reside somewhere within fashionable people's ken; and that ken is, to say the least of it, limited. It is known to vulgarians and common persons that there are buildings beyond Oxford-street on the north side; but it is not known to fashionable people. They, to be sure, know that some "old families" —and this is said with an emphasis which conveys that the families in question are almost pre-Adamite in their age—reside in Portman-square. The fashionable world allows this as a kind of old-world eccentricity, as it allows male

members of said families to appear in the evening
in blue tail-coats and brass buttons, and to swathe
their necks in rolls of cravat, instead of donning
the ordinary small tie.   It is a respectable eccentricity; but it is an eccentricity after all.   North
of Oxford-street is as much "the other side" to
the fashionable world as is Suez to the Eastern
travellers by the Peninsular and Oriental route.
The fashionable world has heard of the big ter-
races of splendid mansions which Messrs. Kelk
and Austin have built in the Bayswater-road
facing the Park; they have seen them occasionally
when they have been driving to Kensington-
gardens; they believe them to be inhabited by a
respectable moneyed class; but the idea of looking
upon them as residences for themselves has never
once struck them.   These houses are such an
enormous distance from "anywhere," which to the
fashionable world is bounded by the Regent-
circus on the east, Belgrave-square on the south,
the Marble Arch on the west, and Oxford-street
on the north.

It is possible that if the choice of district had

been left to Madeleine herself, poor child, she, never particularly caring about such matters, and not being in a very critical or very argumentative state of mind at the period of her marriage, would have fixed upon some comfortable pleasant house, cheerful, roomy, airy, but in a wrong situation. If the choice had been left to her father, there is no doubt that he would have made some tremendous blunder of the like kind; for Kilsyth when in London was always opening his arms and expanding his chest and gasping for air. Accustomed to the free atmosphere of his native Highlands, the worthy gentleman suffered torture in the dull, dead, confined and vitiated air of the London street; and amidst the many sufferings which he underwent for the sake of society during the few weeks when he remained in town was the martyrdom which he was put to in the tiny ill-ventilated rooms in which he had occasionally to dine or pass a ghastly half-hour "assisting" at a reception. But Lady Muriel and Mr. Ramsay Caird took this matter in hand. Of their own express wish it was to them the

task of selecting the residence of the about-to-
be-married couple was to be confided; and there
was no doubt that they would take care that
their choice should not be open to question.

On Squab-street, Grosvenor-place, that choice
fell. A curious street Squab-street; a street in a
progressive state; a street which was feeling the
immediate vicinity of Cubitopolis, but which was
yielding to the advancing conquest piecemeal and
by slow degrees; a street of small houses originally
occupied by small people—doctors, clerks well-up
in the West-end government offices, a barrister
or two with fashionable proclivities, and several
lodging-houses, always filled with good visitors
from the country or eligible regular tenants; a
quiet street, looked upon for many years as being
a long way off, but suddenly awaking to find
itself in the centre of fashion. For while the
doctors had been paying their ordinary seven-and-
sixpenny visits within what was then almost their
suburban neighbourhood; while the West-end
government-office clerks had been plodding to
and fro from their offices; while the barristers

had been pluming themselves on the superiority of
their position to that of their brethren, who, true
to old tradition, had set up their Lares and
Penates in the neighbourhood of Russell-square
and the Foundling Hospital; while the lodging-
house-keeper had vaunted as recommendations the
quietude of the vicinity and the freshness of the
air, the great district now known as Belgravia was
being reclaimed from its native mud, the wild
meadow called the Field of Forty Footsteps was
being drained and built on, the desolate track
over which our ancestors pursued their torchlighted
way to Ranelagh and Vauxhall was being spanned
by arches and undermined with gas-pipes; and
when all these grand improvements were complete, Squab-street, which had held a respectable
but ignominious existence as Squab-street, Pim-
lico, blossomed out in the *Post-Office Directory*
and the *Court-Guide* as Squab-street, S.W., and
thenceforward emerged from its chrysalis state,
and became a recognisable and appreciated butter-
fly.

The effect of the change on the street itself was

immediate. Two or three leases fell in about
that time, and the householders, in whose families
the leases had been for a couple of generations,
made no doubt of their renewal. Lord Battersea
was the ground landlord—not a liberal man, not
a generous man; in short, a screw, and the
driver of a hard bargain, but still a good landlord. He would be all right, of course. Would
he? When the leaseholders went to Lord Battersea's man of business, an apple-faced old gentleman with a white head and a kind of frosty wire
for beard, they learned that his lordship had
fully comprehended the change in the state of
affairs in Squab-street, and was prepared to act
accordingly. As each lease fell in, the house
which was vacant was to be increased by a couple
of stories, and to have its rent trebled. Squab-
street was to be a fitting accessory to Grosvenor-
place. In vain the dispossessed ex-tenants declared that none of his lordship's then holders
could pay the new rent: the apple-faced old
gentleman was sorry; but he thought his lordship
could find plenty of tenants who would. The

tenants grumbled; but the man of business was firm. So were the tenants : they yielded up their leases ; and so the houses were improved, and the rents were raised, and other tenants came of a class hitherto unknown to Squab-street. Married officers of the Guards, who found the situation convenient for Wellington, and not inconvenient for Portman barracks; members of parliament, who found it handy for the House; railway engineers and contractors of fabulous wealth, who could skurry to and fro their offices in Great George-street; and City magnates, who walked to Westminster-bridge, and went humbly in to the Shrine of Mammon by the penny-boat. All these new-comers lived in the enlarged houses, gorgeous stucco-fronted edifices, with porticoes which looked as if they did not belong to the house, but were leaning up against it by accident, and plate-glass windows and conservatories about the size of a market-gardener's hand-lights.

But the other houses in Squab-street, the leases of which had not run out, remained in their normal condition, and were the same little brisk,

cheery, cleanly, snug common brick edifices that
they had been ever since they were built.   The
new style of buildings had grown up round about
them, and was dotted here and there amongst
them ; so that the range of houses in Squab-street
looked like a row of uneven teeth.   The original
settlers, who at first had been rather overawed
by the immigrants, had in time come to look upon
their arrival as rather a benefit than otherwise ;
the doctors extended the number and the importance of their patients ;   the government clerks
bragged judiciously of the " swells" who lived in
their street; and the lodging-house-keepers, secure
with leases of many unexpired years, raised their
prices season after season, and found plenty of
fish to swallow their hooks.

The house which Lady Muriel and Ramsay
Caird, after much driving about, worrying of
house-agents, search of registers, obtaining of
cards to view, and general soul-depression and
leg-weariness,—the house which they eventually
decided upon was represented in the sibylline
books of the agent as an "eligible bachelor's

residence, in that fashionable locality Squab-street, S.W." Such indeed it had been for several previous years; the Honourable Peregrine Fluke, known generally as Fat Fluke, from his tendency to obesity, or Fishy Fluke, from a card transaction in which he had once been mixed up, having been its respected occupant. The Honourable Peregrine Fluke was a very eligible bachelor indeed, and led the life of the gay young fellow and the sad dog until he had passed sixty years of age. Then pale Death, knocking away with impartial rat-tat at the doors of all, the huts of the poor and the castellated turrets of kings, stopped at 122 Squab-street, and called for the Honourable Peregrine Fluke. The eligible bachelor succumbing to the summons, his executors came upon the scene; and wishing to do the best for the lieutenant in the Marines, who was understood to be the eligible bachelor's nephew, but who was clearly proved to be his illegitimate son, put up the lease of the house—the only available thing belonging to the deceased—to auction, and found a purchaser in Kilsyth. Lady Muriel's

clever tact also secured the furniture at a com-
paratively cheap rate. It was not first-rate furniture—a little rococo and old-fashioned; but a
few things could be imported into the drawing-
rooms; and, after all, Ramsay and his wife were
not rich people—young beginners, and that kind
of thing, and the place would do very well to
commence their married life in. Lady Muriel
always spoke of " Ramsay and his wife" when
any monetary question was under debate, ignor-
ing utterly that all the money came from Madeleine's side. For not only was there Madeleine's
twenty thousand pounds, but Kilsyth, when the
marriage was settled, announced his intention of
making the young couple such an allowance as
would prevent his favourite child from missing
any of the comforts, any of the luxuries to which
she had become accustomed.

The situation was undoubtedly fashionable;
but that the house itself might have been more
comfortable could not be denied. What was
complimentarily called the hall, but was really
the passage, was so small, that the enormous

footmen, awaiting the descent of their employ-
ers from the little drawing-rooms above, dared
not house themselves therein. Two of them
would have filled it to overflowing; so they were
compelled either to remain with the carriages, or
to run the chance of being out of the way when
required, and solace themselves in the tap of the
Battersea Arms, down the adjacent mews. The
door was so small and so low, that these great
creatures rubbed their cockades and ruffled their
coats in passing through it. The house stood at
the corner of the mews, and every vehicle that
drove in or out caused an earthquake-like sensa-
tion as it passed. Doors creaked, china rocked,
floors groaned, walls trembled. The little dining-
room was like a red-flocked tank; the little drawing-rooms, encumbered with the newly-imported
extra furniture, were so choke-full, that it was with
the utmost difficulty that visitors could thread their
way between table and couch and ottoman and
étagère. It required a knowledge of the science of
navigation to tack round the piano; and the visitor, when once he had reached a seat by the hostess

near the fireplace, could scarcely devote himself to conversation, owing to the trouble which filled his mind as to how he would ever get away again. It was not advisable to open any of the side-windows, even in the hottest weather, or a stably odour at once pervaded the house, and the forcible language addressed by the grooms to the horses, whose toilet was performed in the open yard, was a little too audible. It was impossible for guests to go through the ceremony of " taking down" to dinner. The steep little ladder-like staircase was only passable by one person at a time; and in the narrow little tank of a dining-room the people who sat with their backs to the fire were roasted alive, and had the additional pleasure of having to eat their meat vegetable-less and sauce-less, there being no approach to them and no passing them. Still everyone said that the situation was delightful, and the house was " quite charming;" and Lady Muriel and Ramsay Caird took great credit to themselves for having secured it.

Madeleine herself was but little impressed by

it. It was immaterial to her where she lived, or
in what style of house. She shrugged her
shoulders when they told her the rooms were
charming; she raised her eyebrows when her
servants complained of darkness and incon-
venience. "It did very well," was her highest
commendation, and she never found fault. If
this girl's life had not been strangely solitary and
without companionship, she would have had all
sorts of confidences to exchange with some half-
dozen intimates as to her new life, her new home,
her new career. As it was, she dropped into it
quietly, with scarcely a remark to any one.
After her little and short-lived day-dream had
dissolved, after she had awakened to the exact
realities which were about her, her period of
suspense was very short. What passed between
her and her brother Ronald at the interview
which, as settled with Lady Muriel, he sought at
his sister's hands was never known. The result
was satisfactory to the prime movers in the scheme;
and the result was that Madeleine was to marry
Ramsay Caird. There was another interview

connected with the matter which neither Lady
Muriel nor Ronald ever heard of. When the
news was first announced to him by his wife,
Kilsyth received it very quietly. The next morning, before my lady had risen, the fond father,
in pursuance of an appointment made in a note
secretly sent up by the maid the night before,
went to his darling's room, and had a half-hour's
long and earnest conversation with her. Earnest
on his side at all events : he asked her whether
this engagement had been brought about of her
own free will; if she had thought over it sufficiently; if she would wish the time of betrothal to
be lengthened beyond the usual period; if there
were anything, in fact, in which she would wish
to make reference to him, and in which he could
aid her. To all these inquiries, urged in the
warmest and most affectionate manner, he got but
the same kind of reply. Madeleine kissed her
father fondly. She hated the thought of leaving
him, she said; but it would do very well. It
would do very well! She had not even the heart
to be deceitful—to feign delight when she did not

feel it. It would do very well! Kilsyth's warm
heart beat more slowly as he listened to this luke-
warm appreciation of the expected joys of his
daughter's future; he scarcely comprehended anything so *fade* and so spiritless from a young girl
about to undergo such an important change in all
the phases of her existence. He again pressed
his question home, and received the same answer;
and then he made up his mind, for the thousandth
time in his life, that women were extraordinary
creatures, and that there was no dealing with
them. This was a very favourite axiom of his,
and had been enounced with much solemnity
frequently. On this occasion, however, he kept
silence, shaking his head in a very thoughtful
and prophetic manner as he descended the stairs
to his own dressing-room. It would do very
well! Madeleine thought of the reply which she
had given to the most important question ever put
to her, after her father had left her and when she
was alone. She knew her father well enough to
be certain that a word spoken at that time by her
to him would have stopped the engagement, and

left her free. And what would then have en-
sued? She would have made an enemy of Lady
Muriel, with whom she had to live; she would
have deeply annoyed Ronald, who had always, in
his odd way, shown the greatest love for her
and the keenest interest in her welfare; and in
the great question of her life she would have
advanced not one whit. Chudleigh Wilmot was
gone—gone for ever. An alliance—a continuance
even of the friendship, such as it had been, with
him was impossible; her friends wanted her to
marry Ramsay Caird. Well, then, it would do
very well!

A phrase significant of a state of mind in
which marriages are often undertaken, but surely
an unlucky and a pitiable state of mind. Something more than a tacit acquiescence is meant by
the vows of the marriage-service; and though
cynics endeavour to persuade us that these vows
are far more frangible and far more often broken
than they used to be, it is as well to believe in the
whole force of them while we stand before the
altar-rails, and before the priest utters his bene-

diction. And the worst of it all was that the phrase expressed Madeleine's feelings thoroughly— her feelings as regarded her marriage, her feelings towards her husband. It *was* Ramsay Caird—it might have been Clement Penruddock, or Frank Only, or Lord Roderick Douglas, or half-a-dozen others. She had an equal liking for all these men ; no love for any one of them. In her earlier girlish days, some year or two beforehand, she had wondered which of the young men who frequented the house would propose to her, and which of them she would marry. None of them had ever proposed to her. They saw long before she did that she was marked down for Ramsay Caird. These sort of things are concealed with the utmost discretion by long-headed mothers, are never suspected by daughters, and are discussed between male friends of the family with much openness and freedom. She had been a favourite with all these pleasant youths ; but they knew perfectly well why Ramsay Caird was always at the house, and why he inevitably had the best chance ; and their regard for Lady Muriel was by no means diminished by the clever manner in which she aided and assisted her protégé.

After marriage, at least during the first few months after marriage, it was very much the same. Madeleine " liked" her husband ; he was quite gentlemanly, genial, cheery, very hospitable, very fond of pleasure, very fond of spending money on her, on himself, on anyone. He never interfered with her in the smallest degree, and never was happier than when she was under the chaperonage of her mother, and his attendance on her was not required. During the first few months of her married life she received a vast number of callers ; all of whose visits she duly repaid ; went out constantly to dinners, balls, receptions of all kinds, to operas and theatres, private and public fêtes,—everywhere, in short, where people can go with decency and enjoy themselves. Not that Madeleine enjoyed herself. " It would do very well," seemed to be the keynote no less in her pleasures than in the rest of her life. In company she sat with the same ever-blank look until she was roused. Then she responded with the same smile. O, so unlike her old smile! With an upward glance of her blue eyes, where there was no light now, and with the little society-laugh which she had recently learned, and which was so different from the hearty ringing burst which used to greet her father's ears at Kilsyth in the old days before her illness—those days which seemed to her, to them all, but to her most of all, so long ago.

Visitors she had in plenty. Scarcely a morning passed without a call from Lady Muriel, who, still priding herself upon the admirable manner in which by her tact her step-daughter had been "settled," looked in to see how she was getting on, to learn who had been to see her during the previous day, what parties she had been to, who she had met, what their reception of her had been, and what invitations for forthcoming gaieties she had received. A comparison of notes on these last matters, now a favourite occupation of Lady Muriel's, with whose great name the world of fashion had begun to busy itself, proclaiming her as one of its leaders,—and she, always equal to the

occasion, had accepted the tribute gracefully, and,
as in everything else, conscientiously discharged
the duties of her position, — then luncheon, to
which meal Lady Muriel would frequently remain,
and when some of the more intimate friends of the
family, notably Mrs. M'Diarmid, would drop in;
not that Mrs. M'Diarmid's accession added much
to the comfort of the meal. The dear old lady,
when her favourite project of marrying Madeleine
to Wilmot had been untimely nipped in the bud,
and when she saw that Ramsay Caird, whom she
cordially disliked, was the accepted suitor, relin-
quished all opposition in silence, and contented
herself with sniffing loudly, as the sole demonstra-
tion of her displeasure. That marriage-service,
which she had pictured to herself with so many
different " eligibles" as bridegrooms, might, but
for the presence of mind of his Right Reverence of
Boscastle, have been sorely interrupted by the de-
fiant sniffs which came from the right-hand pew
close by the altar-rails, where Mrs. Mac, dressed
in the brown *moire* which had so often filled her
dreams, had bestowed herself, to the deep indigna-

tion of the pew-opener. But she did not allow her disapproval of the marriage to interfere with her love for " her dear child ;" she came constantly to Squab-street; and the pleasantest hours of Madeleine's life were passed in the society of this good old woman, when she knew that there was no call upon her to exert herself in any way, or to show herself otherwise than she really was; when she could lie back in her chair, and indulge herself with the sweet sad day-dream of " what might have been," which contrasted so harshly and unsatisfactorily with what was.

A drive in her step-mother's carriage, or a round of calls in her own brougham, filled up the afternoon, until it was time to return home to preside at her tea-table and receive her friends. After her engagement had been regularly announced there had been a good deal of fuss made about that five-o'clock tea-table ; the young men who were intimate at Brook-street had vowed that they would make it the pleasantest in London ; that more news should be heard there than anywhere else ; and that the men who write in the *Cotillon*—a

charming amateur journal of political *canards* and
society gossip, published during the season—should
go on their knees and implore invitations. The
tea-table had been established in due course, but it
had not been such a success as had been anticipated. Madeleine was *triste* and quiet to a degree.
The men could not understand it, she had always
been so pleasant before her marriage; unlike most
women, who are always a doosid sight pleasanter
after it. They had been in the habit of finding
their old partners of the two or three previous
seasons, now married, by no means indisposed to
listen to the compliments which they had been erst
in the habit of addressing to them; and the practice had derived additional piquancy from the fact
of the change of condition in the person addressed.
There was Lady Violet Penruddock, for instance,
only married to old Clem—O, within a few weeks
of Miss Kilsyth's marriage; and how jolly she
was! Looked as fresh as possible—fresh as paint,
some fellow said; but that was a confounded shame,
don't you know,—only a little powder and that
kind of thing, what all girls use, don't you know

—doosid cruel you women are to one another! There was Lady Vi, jolly as a sand-boy! Old Clem was at his club, or some place, and didn't come home till late, and there was always tearing fun at Grosvenor-gate. Charmin' woman, Lady Vi; and very wise of old Clem to like to read the evening papers, and that kind of thing. Not that there was anything to be complained of Caird in this matter; never thought much of Caird, eh, did you? he was never at home; but his wife had grown so confoundedly dull, hipped, and that kind of thing—bored, don't you know? sits still and don't say a word except yes and no; don't help a feller out a bit, you know, and looks rather dreary and dull.

Poor Madeleine! she was beginning to be found out by her friends. If you live in society you must contribute your quota, according to your means—either your rank, your money, your talent—towards the general stock; but unless your birth will warrant it, you must never be dull; and in no case must you differ from the ordinary proceedings of your order. Madeleine was very unlike Lady Violet Penruddock, she felt—very unlike indeed. But that was her misfortune, not her fault. She would have been very glad to laugh and flirt with all her old friends, to talk nonsense and innocent scandal, and all the society chit-chat, if she had been able; but she was not able. Under all her quiet manner and shyness and girlishness Madeleine Caird possessed what Lady Violet Penruddock had never pretended to—a heart. That heart had been hurt and torn and lacerated; and as in the present day it is not possible to explain this, or rather it is considered essential to hide it, Madeleine was obliged to put up with the imputation of dulness, when in reality she was merely suffering from having loved someone who, as she thought, did not care for her, and having been compelled to marry somebody for whom she had no real affection.

Did Ramsay Caird ever fancy that his wife did not care for him, or at least was not as romantically fond of him as are most wives of their husbands during the first few months after marriage? If he did, did the reflection ever cost him a moment's anxiety, a moment's distrust, a thought

that perhaps his own course of living was not precisely adapted to enthral the affections of a young
girl? Not for an instant. Ramsay, when Lady
Muriel's half-spoken hints had first enlightened him
as to the position which, for his dead brother's sake,
her ladyship proposed to him to hold, had cogi-
tated over the matter in an essentially business-
like spirit, and had come to the conclusion that
such an opportunity ought by all means to be made
the most of. He was a calculating cautious young
man, entirely devoid of impulse; and—as had
been suspected by more than one of the frequenters
of the Brook-street establishment, who, however,
were much too good fellows to hint at it openly—
he was a man fond of common, not to say gross
pleasures, which his limited means prevented him
from indulging in. A marriage with Madeleine
Kilsyth, herself a very nice girl, as society girls
went, would give him position, ease, and money—
leave him his own master, with power and opportunity to pursue his own devices—and was therefore for him in every respect most desirable. With
all his easy bearing, his *laissez-aller* manners, and

his apparent *nonchalance*, Mr. Ramsay Caird possessed his full share of the national 'cuteness; and
having made up his mind to win, looked carefully
round him to see where his course lay straightest,
and what shoals were to be avoided. He determined to make a waiting race of it, convinced that
any eagerness or ill-timed enthusiasm might spoil
his chance; he saw that his game was to be quiet
and wait upon his oars until he received the signal
to dash out into mid-stream; his complete willing-
ness to attend to all suggestions, and to take his
time from the family, quite fascinated Ronald Kilsyth, from whom at first Caird had apprehended
opposition; and, as we have seen, when the time
came, he declared himself with so strong a show that
no other competitor dared put in an appearance.

But when the race had been run and the prize
secured, Ramsay Caird felt that the crisis was
past, that the long course of tutelage under which
he had placed himself was at an end, and that
henceforward he would enjoy those benefits for
the acquisition of which he had regulated his conduct for so many months. He had not the smallest

love for his wife ; he had even but small admiration for her looks. Madeleine's blue eyes and golden hair were too cold and insipid for his taste. In his freer moments he was accustomed to talk about "soul"—an attribute which poor Maddy was supposed not to possess—and "liquid eyes" and "classic features" and the "sunny South"— which, as Tommy Toshington remarked, when told of it, accounted for his having seen Caird on the previous Sunday afternoon ringing at the door of the villa temporarily tenanted by Madame Favorita, the *prima donna* of the Opera, and situated in the Alpha-road. Tommy Toshington invariably happened to be passing by when the wrong man was ringing at the wrong house ; and got an immense number of pleasant dinners out of the co-incidence. So that Ramsay Caird saw but little of the interior of his own house after leaving it in the mornings. He at first had been somewhat punctilious and deferential with Lady Muriel, taking care to be at home when she came, and to be in attendance when he thought she would require his presence ; but after a few weeks he threw off this restraint, and kept the hours which suited him. Kilsyth looked blank and uncomfortable once or twice when at dinners, specially given in honour of the new-married couple, Madeleine had appeared alone, and Lady Muriel had proffered a story of Ramsay's toothache or business appointment; and Ronald had looked black, and held more than one muttered conversation with his step-mother, in the course of which his brows contracted, and his mouth grew very rigid. But Madeleine never uttered a word of complaint, although Lady Muriel was in daily expectation of an outburst. She sat quietly, sadly, uninterestedly by. Better, far better, for all concerned if she had had sufficient feeling of her own loneliness, of her own neglected condition, to appeal in language however forcible and strong. To labour under the "it-will-do-very-well" feeling is to be on the high road to destruction.

CHAPTER IV.

INQUISITORIAL.

LADY MURIEL KILSYTH had carried her cherished plan into execution—had seen her wishes as regarded Madeleine and her kinsman Ramsay Caird fulfilled. With wonderfully little trouble, too. When she thought over it all, she was surprised at the apparent ease and rapidity with which the marriage, which she had regarded, after Madeleine's illness at Kilsyth, as a difficult matter to manage, had been brought about. Time had done it all for her—time, assisted by her own tact and skill, and the accomplished fashion after which she had removed all removable obstacles, and availed herself of every circumstance and indication in favour of her cherished project. Nor had the smallest injury to her own position resulted from manœuvering which Lady Muriel would have been ready to blast, if performed by anyone else, with the ruinous epithet, "vulgar matchmaking." No, not the smallest. Indeed, Lady Muriel Kilsyth was one of those fortunate individuals whose position may be generally regarded as, under all circumstances, unassailable. She stood as well with Ronald as ever; and Lady Muriel, with all her imperturbable but never offensive pride, was more anxious about standing well with her step-son than the world would have consented to believe she could have been about securing the good opinion of any human being. She stood, as she always had done, first and chief in the love and esteem of her husband, who, if he did not "understand" her —and he was none the less happy with her that he assuredly did not—made up for his want of comprehension by the most uncompromising trust, devotion, and admiration,—all manifested in his own quiet peculiar way. As this "way" included allowing her the most absolute liberty of action, and an apparent impossibility of questioning her judgment on any conceivable point, it suited Lady Muriel admirably.

Kilsyth was perfectly satisfied with Madeleine's marriage. He believed in love-matches, and it never occurred to him to doubt that this was one. He had quietly taken it for granted, first, because Ramsay Caird had spoken of their " mutual attachment," when he had formally asked Kilsyth for the precious gift of his daughter. Then, Lady Muriel had spoken so warmly of Ramsay's love for Madeleine, had shown such generous and sensitive susceptibility to the possibility of Kilsyth's thinking she had been wrong and injudicious in admitting to such close household intimacy a relative of her own, who was not qualified, as far as fortune was concerned, to pretend to his daughter's hand. Thirdly, if he never doubted Ramsay's being in love with Madeleine—and he never did doubt it for an instant—what could be more natural than that all the young men who had the chance should be in love with Madeleine ? Still less could it have occurred to him to doubt that Madeleine was in love with Ramsay. Ramsay had neither rank nor fortune to give her—that was very certain ; and Kilsyth knew of only two motives as possible incentives to marriage—love and money. Under any circumstances, he never could have suspected his daughter of being actuated by the latter. The fine, gallant, unsophisticated, hearty old fellow, who had had a fair share of happiness all his life, and whose knowledge of human nature was as superficial as his judgment of it was genial, had no notion that pique, thwarted love, blighted hope, wounded pride, the strong and desperate necessity of hiding suffering from kindred household eyes, or an infatuated yearning for the freedom, in certain respects, whose value a man can never estimate, and which a girl gains by her marriage, were among the not unfrequent causes of the taking of that tremendous step. He had never talked to Maddy about her love for Ramsay Caird, certainly; it would never have occurred to him to " make the girl uncomfortable," as he would have expressed it, by any such proceeding; but he would as soon have suspected that Madeleine had brought an asp to her new home among her wedding-clothes as believed that the girl's heart hid, ever so far down in its depths, another image than her husband's.

So Kilsyth was satisfied, in his genial and outspoken way; and Ronald was satisfied, after his grim undemonstrative fashion. And Lady Muriel stood well with all concerned, especially with Madeleine. All the petty restraints of "stepmother" authority, inevitably resented even by the most amiable natures, however mildly exercised, were gone now. Maddy was on a social level with Lady Muriel; there could never more be any of the little discords between them there had been; and Madeleine, as she took her own place in the world, and felt, with a sudden sort of shock, as if she had grown ever so much older, woke up to a fuller consciousness of Lady Muriel's many attractions than she had ever previously attained. She recognised her beauty, her grace, her dignity, her perfect breeding, her thorough *savoir faire* with real appreciation now, and true pleasure and admiration; and one of the happiest thoughts in which she indulged was of how she would be such "good friends" with Lady Muriel, and how she would take her for the model of her conduct, and in every respect her social guide. She was perfectly aware of the dissimilarity which existed between them; and she never would have been guilty of the absurdity of "copying" Lady Muriel's manners, but she might be guided by her for all that. So much the more readily now that she was not always in dread of hearing Wilmot mentioned, of being reminded of him, of exciting a suspicion by some inadvertence that she had been guilty of the folly of thinking he had cared for her just a little. No fear of that now. She was married and *safe*—poor child!

Unsuspicious by nature, ignorant of the world, and unconsciously living a life apart, a life in her own thoughts and reveries, Madeleine was wonderfully indifferent to the conduct of her husband. Either she was really unconscious of it for some time after it had begun to excite the fears of her father, the suspicions of Lady Muriel, the anger of her brother, and the gossip of society, or she successfully contrived to appear so. The judgment of the world leaned to the latter hypothesis; but the

judgment of the world is always uncharitable, and
frequently wrong. In the present instance it was
both. Madeleine did not know that Ramsay Caird
was behaving ill. He was always kind in his
manner to her; and if he was—which there was
no denying—a good deal away from home, why,
he did not differ in that respect from many other
men whom she knew or heard of, and it never
occurred to Madeleine to resent his absence.
Neither did it occur to her to ask herself whether
she was not in real truth rather glad he should
be so much away from her, nor to reflect that the
world, which knew he was, would inevitably come
to one of two conclusions, either that she was a
most unhappy wife, or that she had never loved
her husband.

No; Madeleine Caird thought of none of these
things. She went on her way caring very little
for anything; not entirely unhappy, surprised indeed at the variations in her own spirits, unable to
account for the overwhelming sadness which beset
her at some times, and finding equally inexplicable
the ease with which she flung off this sadness at

others. She was looked at and wondered at and talked of daily by scores of her acquaintances, and she was entirely unconscious that she was the subject of any such scrutiny.

Lady Muriel understood Madeleine's state of mind perfectly. She had a clue to it, which she alone possessed; and while she regarded Ramsay Caird's conduct with all the by no means inconsiderable strength of indignation of which she was capable, she was quite aware that Madeleine was only in the conventional sense an object of compassion.

Was Lady Muriel quite satisfied, was she perfectly content with her success? Hardly so; in the first place, because she was forced to condemn Ramsay Caird, and she did not like to acknowledge the necessity; in the second place, because the result of this success, personal to her, that to which it was to owe its best value, its chief sweetness, was delayed. She chafed at Wilmot's absence now; she had hailed it until Madeleine's marriage had been an accomplished fact; she had tolerated it for a little time afterwards; but now—now her

impatience was undisguised to herself, now she
wanted this man to return—this man who lent her
life such a strange charm, in whose presence the
common atmosphere took a vivid colouring, and
every-day things and occurrences assumed a different meaning and value.

Lady Muriel had heard of Chudleigh Wilmot's
accession to fortune reasonably soon after the
occurrence of the event. Kilsyth happened to be
out of town for a few days on the occasion of Mr.
Foljambe's death, and had therefore not attended
the funeral. General report, at least in Lady
Muriel's particular sphere, had not yet proclaimed
the succession of one unlinked by ties of blood to
the rich banker to the large fortune with which
rumour correctly accredited Mr. Foljambe, and it
remained for Lady Muriel to learn the news from
the same source whence Henrietta Prendergast
had derived the account of Madeleine's marriage.
It was from Mrs. Charlton that Lady Muriel
heard the interesting tidings, and Mrs. Prendergast was present on the occasion. It was the first
time she had ever been in the same room with

Lady Muriel Kilsyth, and she had regarded her with lively curiosity, and much genuine, honest admiration. The finished style of Lady Muriel's beauty—the sort of style which conveys the impression that the possessor of so much beauty is beautiful as much by a sovereign act of her will as by the decree and gift of nature; her grace of manner, true stamp of the *grande dame* set upon her, had irresistible attractions for Henrietta, who was one of those women, by no means so rare as the cynics would have us believe, who can heartily and enthusiastically admire the qualities, physical and mental, of individuals of their own sex.

"I am sure you will be glad to hear the news Mrs. Prendergast has just told us," Mrs. Charlton had said; and then Lady Muriel learned that Mr. Foljambe had made Wilmot his heir. She received the intelligence with the perfection of friendly interest; she turned courteously to Mrs. Prendergast, as though taking it for granted her congratulations were to be addressed to her individually, as Wilmot's relative or friend; and as she did so her heart beat rapidly, with the pulse of one who has escaped a great danger, as she thought, "Had this happened only a few weeks sooner, all might have been lost!"

It was on the same day and at the same hour that Wilmot learned the same fact, from the letter of his dead friend, at Berlin.

Had Lady Muriel been a younger, a weaker, or a less experienced woman, she must inevitably have betrayed some emotion beyond that of mere gratification at a friend's good fortune to the keen eyes of Henrietta Prendergast. But her *savoir faire* was perfect, and she said and looked precisely what she ought to have said and looked. There was a strange accord in the impulsive thoughts of each of these women, so different, so widely separated by circumstances. As Henrietta repeated the intelligence for Lady Muriel's information which she had already communicated to Mrs. Charlton, she too was thinking, "Had this happened only a few weeks sooner, all might have been lost!"

Madeleine's marriage was of no less importance to the designs and the hopes of Henrietta

Prendergast than to those of Lady Muriel Kilsyth.

" I wonder what he will do now ?" said Miss Charlton, who had some of the advantages of silliness, among them a happy *naïveté*, which made it always safe to calculate upon her making some remark or asking some question which others might desire to proffer on their own behalf, but for the restraints of good taste. Lady Muriel could not imagine ; Mrs. Prendergast could not guess. Lady Muriel remarked that Dr. Wilmot would probably be guided by the nature of Mr. Foljambe's property, and the terms of the bequest.

"I fancy the whole property is in money, with the exception of the house in Portland-place," said Henrietta. "I have heard my poor friend- Mrs. Wilmot say that Mr. Foljambe hated all the responsibility of landed property, and had none. So Dr. Wilmot will be free—perhaps he will live altogether abroad."

"Do you think that probable?" said Lady Muriel, very courteously implying Mrs. Prendergast's more intimate acquaintance with the object of the discussion. "For a man of his turn of mind, I fancy there's no place like London —certainly no country like England."

"Ah, yes, Lady Muriel, very true," said the irrepressible Miss Charlton, making her mother wince for the twentieth time since the commencement of the visit; "but then, you see, he has such painful recollections of London.' His poor wife dying as she did, you know, while he was away attending to strangers."

"Very true," said Lady Muriel—with perfect self-possession, and purposely turning her head away from Mrs. Charlton, who glanced angrily and despairingly at her unconscious daughter, and towards Henrietta, who shared her friend's dismay. "We all regretted that circumstance very deeply; and I do not wonder Dr. Wilmot should have felt it as he did: still, he is so strong-minded a man—"

"And so perfectly convinced that it had nothing to do with his wife's death—I mean that he could not have saved her," said Henrietta quickly.

Lady Muriel looked at her inquiringly.

" Mrs. Prendergast was Mrs. Wilmot's intimate friend, and was with her when she died,"
Mrs. Charlton said; and then another visitor
came in, and a *téte-à-téte* established itself between Lady Muriel and Henrietta, which caused
her visit to be prolonged considerably beyond
any former experience of Mrs. Charlton, and gave
her ladyship a good deal to think of, when she
had ordered her coachman to go into the Park,
and gave herself up to her thoughts, mechanically returning the numerous salutes which she
received, and thinking sometimes how strange it
was that there was no one in all this great
crowded London whom it could interest her to
see.

" She must have been a strange woman,"
thought Lady Muriel, " and desperately uninter-
esting, I am sure. That Mrs. Prendergast has
plenty of character. He never mentioned her,
that I can remember; but then he talked so little
of himself, he said so little from which any notion
of his daily life and its surroundings could be

gathered. Yes, I am sure his wife was a tire-
some, commonplace creature, with no kind of
companionship in her—an insipid doll. What
wonderful things one sees under the sun in the
way of unsuitable marriages! To think of such
a man marrying such a woman! But it is
stranger still"—and here Lady Muriel's face
darkened, and a hard look came into her beautiful brown eyes—" it is stranger still to think
that such a man should be attracted by Madeleine—such a merely 'pretty girl.' And he was
—he was; I could not be mistaken. If this fortune had come a little sooner, what would he
have done? He could not of course have proposed to her—impossible in the time—but he
might have told Kilsyth, and gotten his leave,
when the year should be up. What a danger!
I am glad I never thought of such a thing;
I am glad the possibility never occurred to me.
Ronald, indeed, would have been a barrier; but
I need not, I must not deceive myself, Kilsyth
would not have listened to Ronald where Madeleine's happiness was concerned. When will he

return? He must come soon, I suppose, to arrange his affairs. I need not fear his admiration of Madeleine now—he is not a man to admire the woman who could marry Ramsay Caird. If she did betray to him that she loved him, he would have the best and plainest proof in her marriage how fickle and flimsy such a feeling is in her case."

Lady Muriel Kilsyth was in many respects a very superior, in many respects a highly-principled woman; but she had dreamed a forbidden dream, she had cherished a perverse thought, and such speculations as she would once have shrunk from with incredulous amazement had become not only possible but easy to her.

And then all her thoughts directed themselves towards the one object—Wilmot's return. When would he come back? She wrote the news of the disposition of Mr. Foljambe's will to Kilsyth; and he answered in a few jovial lines, expressing his heartfelt satisfaction. She told the news to Madeleine; carelessly, skilfully, opening a large parcel of books as she spoke, and looking at the contents. Madeleine was in her ladyship's boudoir; her bonnet lay on the sofa by her side, and she was idly twisting the strings.

"You are going to fetch Ramsay from the club, are you, Maddy?"

"Yes," said Madeleine listlessly, and looking at the clock; "presently, I suppose. Have you anything new there?"

"New? yes. Good? I can't say. Nothing you would care for, I fancy. All the magazines, though. A new volume by Merivale,—not much after your fashion. A new novel by nobody knows whom—*Squire Fullerton's Will*. By the bye, the name reminds me—I don't think you have heard about Mr. Foljambe's will?"

"No," said Madeleine rising, and tying on her bonnet at the chimney-glass.

"Your father is delighted. Only fancy, Mr. Foljambe has left all his money to Dr. Wilmot."

Madeleine did not answer for a minute. Then she said,

"I am very glad. Was Mr. Foljambe very rich?"

"I believe so. They talk of its being a very large fortune. What a delightful change for Dr. Wilmot! Of course he will give up his profession now, and take a place in society."

"Do you think he would give up his profession for anything, Lady Muriel?" asked Madeleine.

Lady Muriel was standing at a table, still sorting the books; she could not see Maddy's face.

"Give up his profession! Of course, my dear. A man of fortune is not likely to practise as a doctor, I should think; besides, the position."

"Everyone—I mean Mr. Foljambe always said Dr. Wilmot was so devoted to his profession," said Madeleine hesitatingly.

"Of course he was; and of course his friends said so. It is the best and wisest thing a man can have said of him—the best character he can get, while he wants it, and easily laid aside when he doesn't. What's this? *Wine of Shiraz!* O, another book of travels with a fantastical name! Are you going, Maddy? Will you have one of these productions to try?"

" No, thank you," said Madeleine; and she took leave of Lady Muriel, and did not call for Ramsay at the club, but went home, and passed the evening with a book lying open on her knee—a book of which she never turned a page, and wondered when Chudleigh Wilmot would come home. She wondered whether his wealth would make him happy. She wondered whether, if he had been a rich man and not a hard-working doctor, he would have cared a little about her when his wife died; . and whether it was really as Lady Muriel had said, or whether his devotion to his profession was genuine and true. She wondered whether he ever thought of her; she felt sure he knew of her marriage. Well, not *ever*—something forbade her using that word in her thoughts, something told her it would be unjust and unkind; but *much?* Ronald would hear about this bequest of Mr. Foljambe's; would be glad—or sorry—or neither? Supposing it had come earlier, and *he*, Wilmot, had cared for her! would things have been different? would Ronald—But no, no; she must not think of that. Let her still believe he had

seen in her only a patient, only a case of fever,
only an occasion for the exercise of his skill.   She
wondered, if " things had been different"—which
was the phrase by which she translated to herself
" if she had married Wilmot"—whether it would
have harmed anyone; she did not dare to think
how happy it would have made her. Ramsay? But
no; not all the simplicity, not all the credulous
egotism of girlhood—and Madeleine had her fair
share of those natural qualities—could persuade
her that Ramsay's life would have been marred if
their marriage had never taken place.   And so she
wondered and wondered, recurring often in her
thoughts solemnly to the dead woman who had
been Wilmot's wife, and thinking sadly, wonder-
ingly, over that life, all unknown to her; and yet
concerning which some mysterious instinct had
whispered to her vaguely and unhappily.   She
hoped people would not talk much to her, or before her, of this bequest of Mr. Foljambe's.   It
embarrassed her, though she knew it ought not;
who ought to be so ready as she to speak of him,
to whom no one owed so much?

Henrietta Prendergast wondered too when Dr.
Wilmot would return to London; and questioned
Dr. Whittaker, who had contrived in a wonderfully brief space of time to accumulate an extraordinary quantity of information relative to the
nature and extent of Wilmot's inheritance.   The
worthy man possessed an inherent talent for gossip,
which was likely to be of great service to him in
his career, being admittedly an immense recom-
mendation for a physician, especially when his
practice lies in a class of society largely productive of *malades imaginaires*.   Wilmot was left at
perfect liberty, except in the matter of the house in
Portland-place.   It was not to be sold; and Wilmot had instructed the solicitors to keep up the
establishment, and retain the old housekeeper and
butler permanently in his service.   As for his
old house in Charles-street, Wilmot had behaved
most generously indeed — Dr. Whittaker would
say he had placed it entirely at his disposal nobly:
for the remainder of his lease; and by the time
that should expire, he had expressed his conviction
that Dr. Whittaker would be making his fortune. '

" All the more chance of it, Mrs. Prendergast,"
said Whittaker with his smoothest smile, " that
Wilmot will be out of my way; he's a wonderfully clever fellow, wonderfully; and I can't imagine a more popular physician. I assure you he
reminds me, in his way of dealing with a case, of
Carlyle's description of Frederick the Great's eyes,
' rapidity resting upon depth.' Quite Wilmot—
quite Wilmot, I assure you." And Dr. Whittaker,
considering that he had made a remarkably good
hit, took himself off, leaving Henrietta with new
matter for her thoughts.

The three women who thus pondered and thought
and speculated about Chudleigh Wilmot had plenty
of time during which to indulge in these vain occupations. Time passed on, and Mr. Foljambe's heir
did not present himself to the tide of congratulations which awaited him. The first interest of the
intelligence died out. Other rich men died, and
left their wealth to other heirs expectant or non-
expectant. " Foljambe's will " and " Wilmot's
luck" had almost ceased to be talked about when

Chudleigh Wilmot ventured into society. Henrietta Prendergast was the first of the three who saw him. As for Lady Muriel and Madeleine, they were less likely to meet him than any women in London; for the good reason that Wilmot sedulously avoided them. And for a time successfully; but that was not always to be. He believed that the page of the book of his life on which " Madeleine Kilsyth" was written was closed for ever; Fate had written upon another, " Madeleine Caird."

CHAPTER V.

OF all those who were in the habit of seeing Madeleine under circumstances which made it possible for them to observe her closely, her brother had been the last to perceive and the most reluctant to acknowledge that the state of her health was far from satisfactory. Ronald Kilsyth was habitually unobservant in matters of the kind; and he usually saw Madeleine in the evening, when the false spirits and deceptive flush of her disease produced an appearance of health and vivacity which might have imposed upon a closer observer. He knew she had a cough indeed ; but then " Maddy always had a cough — I never remember her without one," was the ready reply to any observations made on the subject in his hearing, and to any misgivings which occasionally flitted across his own

mind. It did not occur to him that in this " fact"
there was no reply at all, but rather an additional reason for apprehension concerning this
cough. When Madeleine was a child, it was
acknowledged that she was delicate. " She had
it from her poor mother," Kilsyth would say—
Kilsyth, who never had a day's illness in his life,
and in whose family ninety years was considered
a fair age. But she was to get strong, to " out-
grow her delicacy" as she grew up. When
Madeleine was a girl, she was still delicate; perhaps more continuously so than she had been as a
child, though no longer subject to the maladies of
childhood; but she was to get stronger as she
grew older. Now Madeleine had grown older;
the delicate girl, with her fragile figure and
poetical face, was no more; in her place was a
beautiful, self-possessed young woman—a wife,
with a place in the world, and a career before her.
Strange, but Madeleine was still delicate; the
time unhesitatingly foretold, looked forward to so
anxiously with a kind of weary patience by her
father, had come; but it had not brought the

anticipated, the desired result. Madeleine was more delicate than ever. Her friends saw it, her father saw it; her step-mother saw it more clearly than either—saw it with feelings which would have been remorseful, had she not arrested their tendency in that direction by constantly reminding herself that Madeleine had been delicate as a child and as a girl; but her brother had not permitted the fact to establish itself in his mind.

The old affection, tacitly interrupted for a time, when Madeleine had felt the unexpressed opposition of her brother to Chudleigh Wilmot, had been as tacitly restored between them since Madeleine's marriage. She had felt during that sad interval, all whose sadness was hidden and unspoken, never taking an external shape, but formless, like a sorrow in a dream, that circumstances and her surroundings were stronger than she was; she had felt somewhat like a prisoner, against and for whom conspiracies were formed, but who had no power to meddle in them, and no distinct knowledge of their methods or objects. Mrs. M'Diarmid, she vaguely felt, was for her, in

the secret desire of her heart; her brother against
her. Ronald would have been successful in any
case, she had been quite sure, even if he had not
been at once justified and relieved of all apprehen-
sions by Wilmot's departure. He did not care for
her—he had gone away; they might each and all
have spared the pains they had taken—their bug-
bear had been only a myth. Then Madeleine, in
whose mind justice had a high place, turned again
to her brother as tacitly, as completely, without
explanation, as she had turned from him, and loved
him, admired him, thought about him, and clung
to him as she had been wont to do. Which surprised Ronald Kilsyth, who had taken it for
granted that Madeleine, who had married Ramsay
Caird a good deal to the Captain's surprise—who
had his theories concerning affinities and analo-
gies, into which this alliance by no means fitted—
but not at all to his displeasure, would discard
everybody in favour of her husband, and devote
herself to him after the gushing fashion of very
young brides in ordinary. He had smiled grimly
to himself occasionally, as he wondered whether

Lady Muriel would be altogether satisfied with a match which was so largely of her own bringing about, and by which, whatever advantages she had secured to her own family, for whom she entertained a truly clannish attachment, she had undeniably provided herself with a young, beautiful, and ever-present rival in her own queendom of fashion and social sway. "Let them fight it out," Captain Kilsyth had thought; "it would have been pleasanter if Maddy had gone farther afield; but it cannot be helped. I am sure she is glad to get away from Lady Muriel; and I am sure Lady Muriel is glad to get rid of her. I don't understand her taking to Caird in this way; for I am as strongly convinced as ever it was no false alarm about Wilmot; she was in love with him; only," and his face reddened, "thank God, she did not know it. However, it is time wasted to wonder about women, even the best and the truest of them, and no very humiliating acknowledgment to say I cannot understand them."

But Captain Kilsyth was destined to find himself unable to discard reflection on his sister and

her marriage after this fashion. Madeleine put
all his previously conceived ideas to rout, and dis-
concerted all his expectations. She was by no
means engrossed by her husband; she did not
assume any of the happy fussiness or fussy happiness which he had observed exhibit themselves
in *jeunes ménages* constructed on the old-fashioned
principle of love, as opposed to the modern ex-
pedient of *convenance*. She was just as friendly,
just as kindly with Ramsay Caird as she had been
in the days before their brief engagement, in the
days when Ronald had found it difficult to believe that Lady Muriel's wishes and plans would
ever be realised. She did not talk about her
house, or give herself any of the pretty "mar-
ried-woman" airs which are additional charms
in brides in their teens. She led, as far as
Ronald knew, much the same sort of life she
had led under her step-mother's chaperonage; and
Kilsyth visited her every day: Ronald too, when
he was in town; and he soon felt that he was
all to her he had formerly been. The innocent,
girlish, loving heart had room and power for

grief indeed, but none for a half-understood anger, none for the prolongation of an involuntary estrangement. So the first months of Madeleine's married life were pleasant to her brother in his relations with her; and the first thing which occurred to trouble his mind in reference to her was his suspicion and dislike of certain points in Ramsay Caird's conduct. Here, again, Madeleine puzzled him. Naturally, he had no sooner conceived this suspicious displeasure against the man to whom such an immense trust as that of his sister's happiness had been committed than he sought to discover by Madeleine's looks and manner whether and how far her happiness was compromised by what he observed. But he failed to discover any of the indications which he sought. Madeleine's spirits were unequal, but her disposition had never been precisely gay; and there was no trace of pique, sullenness, or the consciousness of offence in her manner towards her husband.

It was when Ronald's indignation against Ramsay Caird was rising fast, and he began to

think Madeleine either unaccountably indifferent
to certain things which women of quite as gentle
a nature as hers would inevitably and reasonably resent, or that she was concealing her sen-
timents, in the interests of her dignity, with a
degree of skill and cleverness for which he was
far from having given her credit, that his sister's delicate health for the first time attracted
Ronald's attention. And Mrs. M'Diarmid was
the medium of the first communication on the
subject which alarmed him.

As in all similar cases, attention once excited,
anxiety once awakened, the progress of both is
rapid. Ronald questioned his father, questioned
Lady Muriel, questioned Ramsay Caird. In each
instance the result was the same. Madeleine
was undoubtedly very delicate, and the danger
of alarming her, which, as her organisation was
highly nervous and sensitive, was considerable,
presented a serious obstacle to the taking of the
active measures which had become undeniably
desirable.

One day Ronald went to see his sister earlier

in the day than usual, having been told by Mrs. M'Diarmid that her looks in the evening were not by any means a reliable indication of the state of her health. He found her lying on a sofa in her dressing-room, wholly unoccupied, and with an expression of listless weariness in her face and figure which even his unskilled judgment could not avoid observing and appreciating with alarm.

One hand was under her head, the other hung listlessly down; and as Ronald drew near, and took it in his tenderly, he saw how thin the fingers were, how blue the veins, how they marked their course too strongly under the white skin, and how the rose-tint was gone. As he took the gentle hand, he felt that it was cold; but it burned in his clasp before he had held it a minute. Like all men of his stamp, Ronald Kilsyth, when he was touched, was deeply touched; when his mood was tender, it was very tender. Madeleine looked at him; and the love and sadness in her smile pierced at once his well-defended heart.

"What's this I hear, Maddy, about your not being well?" he said, as he seated himself beside her sofa, and kissed her forehead—it was slightly damp, he felt, and she touched it with her handkerchief frequently while he stayed. "You were not complaining last week, when I saw you last; and now I've just come up to town, and been to Brook-street, I find my father and my lady quite full of your not being well. What is it all, Maddy? what are you suffering from, and why have you said nothing about it?"

"I am not very ill, Ronald," said Madeleine, raising herself, and propping herself up on her cushions by leaning on her elbow, one hand under her head, its fingers in her golden hair; more profuse and beautiful than ever Ronald thought the hair was. "I am really not a bit worse than I have been; only I suddenly felt a few days ago that I could not go on making efforts, and going out, and seeing people, and all that kind of thing, any longer; and then papa got uneasy about me. I assure you that is the only differ-

ence; and you know it does grow horribly tire-
some, dear, don't you? At least you don't know,
because you never would do it; and you were
right; but I—I hadn't much else to do, and
it does not do to seem peculiar; and I went on as
long as I could. But this last week was really too
much for me, and I had to tell Lady Muriel I
must be quiet; and so I have been quiet, lying
here."

She gave her brother this simple explanation,
her blue eyes looking at him with a smile, and a
tone in her voice as though she prayed him not to
blame her.

"My poor child, my darling Maddy!" said
Ronald, "to think of your trying to go on in that
way, and feeling so unequal to it, and fancying
all the time you must! What a wonderful life of
humbug and delusion you women lead, to be sure,
either with your will or against it! Now tell me,
does Ramsay know how ill you are, and how you
have been doing all sorts of things which are most
unfit for you, until you are quite worn out?"

"Ramsay is very kind," said Madeleine; and

then she hesitated, and the colour deepened painfully in her face; "but you know, Ronald, men are not very patient with women when they are only ailing; if I were seriously ill, it would be quite a different thing. He really is not in the least to blame," she went on hurriedly; "he gets bored at home, you know; and since I have not been feeling strong, it has been quite a relief to me to be alone."

"I see—I understand," said Ronald; but his tone did not reassure Madeleine.

"You really must not blame him," she repeated. "You know *you* yourself did not perceive that I was ill before you went away; and it is only within the last week, I assure you. I suppose the cough has weakened me; for some time, in the morning, I have felt giddy going downstairs, so I thought it better not to try it until I get stronger."

"I have not heard you cough much, Madeleine, that is, not more than usual, you know. You have always had a cough, more or less."

"Yes," said Madeleine simply, "ever since I

was born, I believe; but it is never really bad, except in the morning, and sometimes at night. Up to this time I have got on very well in the day and the afternoon; and I like the evening best of all, if I am not too tired. I feel quite bright in the evening, especially when I take my drops."

" What drops, Maddy ?"

" The drops Sir Saville Rowe ordered for me last winter," said Madeleine. " I got on very well with them, and I don't want anything else. Papa wants me to see some of the great doctors, but there's really no occasion; and I hate strangers. Dr. Whittaker comes occasionally—as Sir Saville wished—and he does well enough. The mere idea of seeing a stranger now—in that way— would make me nervous and miserable." Indeed she flushed up again, looked excited and feverish, and a violent fit of coughing came on, and interrupted any remonstrance on Ronald's part, which perhaps she dreaded.

But she need not have dreaded such remonstrance. There was a consciousness in Ronald's heart which kept him silent; and besides, with every word his sister had spoken, with every instant during which his examination of her, close though furtive, had lasted, increasing alarm had taken firmer hold of him. How had he been so blind? How had he been content to accept appearances in Madeleine's case? how had he failed to search and examine rightly into the story of this marriage, and satisfy himself that his sister's heart was in it, that she had really forgotten Wilmot? For a conviction seized upon Ronald Kilsyth, as he looked at his sister and listened to her, that had she been really happy, this state of things would not have existed. In the angry and suspicious state of his feelings towards Wilmot, he had accorded little attention, and less credence, to his father's confidences respecting Wilmot's opinion and warnings about Madeleine's health. He was too honourable, too true a gentleman, even in his anger to set down Wilmot as insincere, as acting like a charlatan or an alarmist; but he had dismissed the matter from his thoughts with disregard and impatience. How awfully, how fatally wrong he had been! And a flame of anger sprung wildly up in

his heart; anger which involved equally himself
and Lady Muriel.

Yes, Lady Muriel! All he had thought and
done, he had thought and done at her instigation;
and though, when Ronald thought the matter over
calmly afterwards, as was his wont, he was unable to believe that any other course than that
which had ended in the complete separation of
Wilmot and Madeleine would have been possible,
still he was tormented with this blind burning
anger.

When Lady Muriel had aroused his suspicions,
had awakened his fears, Wilmot was a married
man; but when he had acted upon these fears
and suspicions, Wilmot's wife was dead. "It
might have been," then he thought. True; but
would he not, being without the knowledge, the
fear which now possessed him, have at any time,
and under any circumstances, prevented it? It
cost him a struggle now, when the knowledge and
the fear had come, and his mind was full of them,
to acknowledge that he would; but Ronald was
essentially an honest man—he made the struggle

and the acknowledgment. In so far he had no
right to blame Lady Muriel.

In so far—but what about Ramsay Caird?
How had that marriage been brought about?
How had his sister been induced to marry a man
whom he now felt assured she did not love?—something had revealed it to him, nothing she had
said, nothing she had looked. How had this
marriage, by which his sister had not gained in
rank, wealth, or position, been brought about?
(He thought at this stage of his meditations, with
a sigh, that Wilmot could even have given her
wealth now—how *bizarre* the arrangements of fate
are!) How had that been done? By Lady
Muriel of course, and no other. Maddy might
have remained contentedly enough at home, might
have been suffered gradually to forget Wilmot,
and enticed into the amusements and distractions
natural to her age and position; there was no need
for this extreme measure of inducing her to fix
her fate precipitately by a marriage with Ramsay
Caird. Yes, Lady Muriel had done it; done it to
secure Madeleine's fortune to a relative of her

own, and to disembarrass herself of a grown-up
step-daughter. How blind he had been, how
completely he had played into her hands! Thus
thought Ronald, as he strode about his bare room
at Brook-street, his face haggard with care, and
his heart sick with the terrible fear which had
smitten it with his first look at Madeleine.

Ronald's interview with his sister had been
long and painful to him, though nothing, or very
little more, had been said on the subject of her
health. He had perceived her anxiety to abridge
discussion on that point, and had fallen in with
her humour. Once or twice, as he talked with
her, he had asked her if she was quite sure he was
not wearying her, if she did not feel tired or in-
clined to sleep, if he should go, and send her maid
to her. But to all his questions she replied no;
she was quite comfortable, and had not felt so
happy for a long time; and she had begged him to
stay with her as long as he could. The brother
and sister talked of numerous subjects—much of
Kilsyth, and their childhood; a little of their
several modes of life in the present; and sometimes

the current of their talk would be broken by
Madeleine's low musical laugh, but oftener by the
miserable cough, from which Ronald shrunk ap-
palled, wondering that he ever could have heard it
without alarm, with indifference. But the truth
was, he had never heard it at all. The cough had
changed its character; and the significance which
it had assumed, and which crept coldly with its
hollow sound to Ronald's heart, was new.

Ronald had a dinner engagement for that day,
and remained with his sister until it was time to
go home and dress. He looked into Kilsyth's
room on his way to the hall-door, when he had
completed that operation; but his father was not
there. "I will speak to him in the morning,"
thought Ronald. "I was impatient with him for
croaking, as I thought, about Maddy. God help
him, I'm much mistaken, or it's worse than he
thinks for."

And so Captain Kilsyth went out to dinner,
and was colder in his manner and much less lucid
and decisive in his conversation than usual. He
left the party early, did not "join the ladies;" and

all the other guests, notably "the ladies" themselves, were of opinion that they had no loss.

"If Wilmot had not gone away when he did,"
said Kilsyth to his son, at an advanced stage of
the long and sad conversation which took place
between them on the following morning, " Maddy
would have been quite well now. Nobody understood her as he did; you must have seen it to
have believed it, Ronald. You always had some
unaccountable prejudice against Wilmot—I could
not get to the bottom of it—but you must have
acknowledged *that*, if you had seen it."

"It is too late to talk about that now, sir,"
said Ronald; "and you are quite mistaken in
supposing that I undervalue Dr. Wilmot's ability.
But something decisive must be done at once; and
as Wilmot's advice is not to be had, we must procure the best within our reach. There is no use
now in looking back; but I do wonder Caird has
permitted her to be without good advice all this
time, and has suffered us to be so misled. He
must have known of the cough being so bad in

the morning, and of her exhaustion at times when neither you nor Lady Muriel saw her." .

Kilsyth sighed. "I spoke to him yesterday," he said, "and I found him very easy about the matter. He says Maddy wouldn't have a strange doctor."

"Maddy wouldn't have a strange doctor! My dear father, what perfect nonsense! As if Maddy were the proper person to judge on such a subject —as if she ever ought to have been asked or consulted! As if anyone in what I fear is her state ever had any consciousness of danger! I recognise Caird completely in that, his invincible easiness, his selfishness, his—"

He stopped. Kilsyth was looking at him, new concern and anxiety in his face; and Ronald had no desire to cause either, beyond the absolute necessity of the case, to his father.

"However," he said, "let us at least be energetic now. Come with me to see her now, and then we will consult someone with a first-rate reputation. Maddy will not offer any resistance when she sees your anxiety, and knows your wishes."

Kilsyth and his son walked out together; and in the street he took Ronald's arm. He was changed, enfeebled, by the fear which had captured him a few days since, and held him inexorably in its grasp.

Madeleine received her father and brother cheerfully. As usual now, she was in her dressing-room, and also, as usual, she was lying down. Ramsay Caird had told her the previous evening that her father was anxious she should have immediate advice, and she was prepared to accede to the wish. Not that she shared it; not that, as Ronald supposed, she was unconscious of her danger, as consumptive persons usually are. Quite the contrary, in fact. Madeleine Caird firmly believed that she was dying; only she did not in the least wish to live; and neither did she wish that her father should learn the fact before it became inevitable, which she felt it must, so soon as an experienced medical opinion should be taken upon her case.

But a certain dulness of all her faculties had made itself felt within the last few days, and she was particularly under its influence just then. She had neither the power nor the inclination to combat any opinion, to dissent from any wish. So she said, "Certainly, papa, if it will make your mind any easier about me;" and twined her thin arm round her father's neck and kissed him, when he said, "I may bring a doctor to see you then, my darling, and you will tell him all about yourself."

Her arm was still about his neck, and his brow was resting against her cheek, when he said:

"Ah, if Wilmot were only here! No one ever understood you like Wilmot, my darling."

Neither Ronald nor Madeleine said a word in reply; and when Ronald took leave of his sister, he avoided meeting her glance.

CHAPTER VI.

ICONOCLASTIC.

In this great London world of ours it is our boast that we live free and unfettered by the opinions of our neighbours; that we may be unacquainted with those persons who for a score of years have resided on either side of us; that our sayings and doings, our "goings on," the company we keep, the lives we lead, and the pursuits we follow, are nothing to anybody, and are consequently unnoticed. We pride ourselves on this not a little; we shrug our shoulders and elevate our eyebrows when we talk of the small scandal and the petty spite of provincial towns; we are grateful that, in whatever state the larger vices may be, the smaller ones, at all events, do not flourish among us; and, in short, we take to ourselves enormous credit for the possession of something which has not the slightest real

existence, and for the absence of something else
which is of daily growth. It is true that in
London a man need not be particular about the
shape of his hat or the cut of his coat, so
far as London itself is concerned, any more than
he need fear that his having taken too much
wine at a public dinner, or held a lengthened
flirtation with a barmaid, will appear in the public
prints; but in his own circle, be it high or low,
large or small, pharisaical or liberal-minded, as
much attention will be paid to all he does, his
speeches, actions, and mode of life will be the subject of as much spiteful comment, as if he lived at
Hull or vegetated at York. The insane desire to
talk about trifles, to indulge in childish chit-chat
and terrible twaddle, to erect mole-hills into moun-
tains, and to find spots in social suns, exists everywhere amongst people who have nothing to do,
and who carry out the doctrine laid down by Dr.
Watts by applying their " idle hands" to " some
mischief still." The Duke of Dilworth, interested
in the management of his own estates, looking
after the race-horses under his trainer's care

hunting up his political influence, and seeing that it sustains no diminution, marking catalogues of coming picture-sales for purchases which he has long expected must enter the market, devising alterations in his Highland shooting-box, planning yachting expeditions, going through, in fact, that business of pleasure which is the real business of his life, has no time for profitless talk and ridiculous gossip, which, as his grace says, " he leaves for women." But the women like what is left for them. The Duchess and the Ladies Daffy have none of these occupations to fill the " fallow leisure of their lives"—their calls and visits, their fête-attendances and garden-parties, their play at poor-visitings and High-Church-service frequentings, leave them yet an enormous margin of waste time, which is more or less filled up by tattle of a generally derogatory nature. It is the same in nearly every class of life : men must work, and women must talk ; and when they talk, their conversation is robbed of half its zest and point if it be not disparaging and detrimental to their dearest friends.

It was not to be imagined that the Ramsay-
Caird *ménage*, even had it been very differently
constituted, could have escaped criticism; as it
was, it courted it. The mere fact of Ramsay Caird
himself having somehow or other slipped into the
society of *nous autres* (it was solely through the
Kilsyths that he was known in the set), and having had the audacity to carry away one of the
prizes, would in itself have attracted sufficient attention to him and his, had other inducements been
wanting. But other inducements were not wanting. The alteration which had taken place in
Madeleine since her illness in Scotland, more
especially since the time of the announcement
of her engagement, was matter of public comment; and all kinds of stories were set afloat by
her dearest friends to account for it. That she
had had some dreadful love-affair, highly injudicious, impossible of achievement, was one of the
most romantic; and being one of the most mis-
chievous, consequently became one of the most
popular theories, the only difficulty being to find
for this desperate affair—which, it was said, had

superinduced her illness, scarlet-fever being, as is well known to the faculty, essentially a mental disease—a hero. The list of visitors to the house was discussed in half-a-dozen different places; but no one at all likely to fill the character could be found, until Colonel Jefferson was accidentally hit upon. This, coupled with the fact that Colonel Jefferson's mad pursuit of Lady Emily Fairfax, which everyone knew had so long existed, had ceased about that time, was extensively promulgated, and pretty generally accepted. So extensively promulgated, that it reached the ears of Colonel Jefferson himself, and elicited from him an expression of opinion couched in language rather stronger than that gallant officer usually permitted himself the use of—to the effect that, if he found anyone engaged in the fetching and carrying of such infernal lies, he, Colonel Jefferson, should make it his business to inflict personal chastisement on him, the said fetcher and carrier. A representation of this kind coming from a very big and strong man, who in such matters had the reputation of keeping his promise, had the effect of doing away with all identification of Mrs. Ramsay Caird's supposed heartbroken lover, and of restoring him his anonymity, but the fact of his existence still was whispered abroad; else why had one of the brightest girls of the past season—not that there was ever anything in her very clever, or that she was ever anything but extremely " missy," but still a pleasant, cheerful kind of girl in her way—why had she become dull and *triste*, and obviously uncaring for anything? That was what society wanted to know.

As for her husband, as for Ramsay Caird, society's tongue said very little about him; but society's shoulders, and eyebrows, and hands, and fluttering fans, hinted a' great deal. Society was divided on the subject of Mr. Ramsay Caird. One portion of it threw out nebulous allusions to the fascinations of Madame Favorita of the Italian Opera, suggested the usual course pursued by beggars who had been set upon horseback, wondered how Madeleine's relations could endure the state of things which existed under

their very eyes, and thought that the time could
not be very far distant when Captain Kilsyth—
who had the name, as you very well know, my
dear, for being so very particular in such matters,
not to say strait-laced—would call his brother-
in-law to account for his goings on. The other
portion of society was more liberal, so far at
least as the gentleman was concerned. What, it
asked, was the position of a man who found his
newly-married wife evidently preoccupied with
the loss of some previous flirtation? What was
to be expected from a man who had found Dead-
Sea apples instead of fruit, and utter indifference
instead of conjugal love and domestic happiness?
The *nous-autres* feeling penetrated into the discussion. It was not likely that a young man
who had been brought up in a different sphere,
who had been, if what people said was correct,
a clerk or something of the kind to a lawyer in
Edinburgh, could comprehend the necessity for
such a course of conduct under the circumstances
as the belonging to their class would naturally
dictate. If Mr. Caird had made a mistake—

well, mistakes were often made, often without
getting the equivalent which he, in allying himself with an old family in the position of the
Kilsyths, had secured for himself.   But they were
always borne *sub silentio*—at all events the sufferer, however he might seek for distraction in
private, did not let the mistake which he had
made, and the means he had adopted for his
own compensation, become such common gossip-
matter for the world at large.

Such conversation as this is not indulged in
without its reaching the ears of those most concerned.   When one says most concerned, one means
those likely to take most concern in it.   It is
doubtful if Madeleine's ears were ever disturbed
by any of the rumours in which she played so
prominent a part.   It is certain that her husband
never knew of the interest which he excited in so
many of his acquaintances; equally certain that if
he had known it, the knowledge thus gained would
not have caused him an emotion.   Lady Muriel,
however, was fully acquainted with all that was
said.   The world, which did her homage as one

of its queens of fashion, took every possible occasion to remind her that she was mortal, and
found no better opportunity than in pointing out
the mistake which she had made in the marriage of her step-daughter and the settlement in
life of her *protégé*. Odd words dropped here
and there, sly hints, innuendoes, phrases capable of double meaning, and always receiving the
utmost perversion which could be employed in
their warping, nay, in some instances, anony-
mous letters—the basest shifts to which treachery
can stoop,—all these ingredients were made use
of for the poisoning of Lady Muriel's cup of life,
and for the undermining of that pinnacle to which
society had raised her.

Nor was Ronald Kilsyth ignorant of the
world's talk and the world's expressions. Isolate
himself as much as he would, be as self-contained
and as solitary as an oyster, fend off confidence,
shut his ears to gossip,—all he could do was to
exclude pleasant things from him; the unpleasant
had penetrating qualities, and invariably made
their way. He knew well enough what was said

in every kind of society about Mr. and Mrs.
Ramsay Caird. When he dined áway from the
mess, he had a curiously unpleasant feeling that
advantage would be taken of his absence to
discuss that unfortunate *ménage*. When he dined
at his club, he had a morbid horror lest the two
men seated at the next table should begin to talk
about it. The disappointment about the whole
thing had been so great as to make him morbidly
sensitive on the point, to ascribe to it far greater
interest than it really possessed for the world in
general, and to allow it to prey on his mind, and
seriously to influence his health. It had been
such a consummate failure! And he, as he
owned to himself,—he was primarily responsible
for the marriage! If Lady Muriel had not had
his assistance, she would never have carried her
point of getting Madeleine for Ramsay Caird;
one word from him would have nipped that acquaintance in the bud, would have stopped the
completion of the project, no matter how far it
had advanced. And he had never said that
word. Why? He comforted himself by think-

ing that Caird had never shown himself in his
real character before his marriage; but the fact
was, although Ronald would not avow it, that he
had been hoodwinked by the deference so deftly
paid to him both by his step-mother and her
confederate, who had consulted him on all points,
and cajoled him and used him as a tool in their
hands. He thought over all this very bitterly
now; he saw how he had been treated, and
stamped and raved in impotent fury as he remembered how he had been led on step by step, and
how weak and vacillating he must have appeared
in a matter in which he was most deeply interested,
and which, during the whole of its progress, he
thought he was managing so well.

To no man in London could such a *fiasco* as
his sister's marriage had turned out be more
oppressively overwhelming, productive of more
thorough disgust and annoyance than to Ronald
Kilsyth. The *fiasco* was so glaring, that at once
two points on which the young man most prided
himself stood impugned. Everyone knew that
dear old Kilsyth himself would not have inter-

fered in such a matter, and that the final settlement of it, after Lady Muriel's light skirmishing
had been done, must have been left to Ronald,
who was the sensible one of the family. He had
then, in the eyes of the world, either had so little
care for his sister's future as to sanction her
marriage with a very ineligible man, or so little
natural perspicacity and sharpness as to be deceived by such a shallow pretender as Caird.
That anyone should entertain either of these suppositions was gall and wormwood to Ronald.
He whose reputation for clear - headedness and
far-seeing had only been equalled by the esteem in
which by all men he had been held for his strict
honesty and probity and the Spartan quality of his
virtue,—that he should be suspected—more than
suspected, in certain quarters accused—of folly or
want of proper caution where his sister was concerned, was to him inexpressibly painful. Perhaps the worst thing of all was to know that
people knew that he was aware of what was
said, and that he suffered under the tittle-tattle
and the gossip. He tried to forget that idea, to

dispel and do away with it by changing his usual habits; he went about; he was seen—for one week —oftener in society than he had been for months previously: but the morbid feeling came upon him there; he fancied that people noticed his presence, and attributed it to its right cause; that every whisper which was uttered in the room had Madeleine for its burden; that the whole company had their minds filled with him, and were thinking of him either pityingly, sarcastically, or angrily, according to their various temperaments.

He avoided Brook-street at this time as religiously as he avoided the little residence in Squab-street. He did not particularly care about meeting his father, though he thought Kilsyth would probably know nothing of what so many were talking of; and he had resolutely shunned a meeting with Lady Muriel, for Ronald in his inmost heart did his step-mother a gross injustice. He fully believed that she was perfectly cognisant of Ramsay Caird's real character; whereas, in truth, no one had been more astonished at what her *protégé* had proved himself than Lady Muriel—

and very few more distressed.   Ronald, however,
thought otherwise; and being a gentleman, he carefully avoided meeting her ladyship, lest he might
lose his temper and forget himself.   The Kilsyth
blood *was* hot, and even in the heir to the name
there had been occasions when it was pretty nearly
up to boiling-point.

For the same reason he avoided all chance of
running across his brother-in-law.   In common
with most men of strong feelings always kept in
a state of repression, Ronald Kilsyth was particularly sensitive; and the idea of the publicity already
accruing to this wretched business being increased
by any possible tattle of open rupture between
members of the family horrified him dreadfully.
If he did not dare trust himself with Lady Muriel, he should certainly have to exercise a much
stronger command over himself in the event of his
ever meeting Ramsay Caird.   Every governing
principle of his life rose up within him against
that young man; and on the first occasion of his
hearing—accidentally, as men often hear things of
the greatest import to themselves—of Mr. Caird's

doings, Ronald Kilsyth had for the whole night paced his barrack-room, trying in every possible form to pick such a quarrel with Caird as might leave no real clue to its origin, and enable him to work out his revenge without compromising any-one. But he soon saw the futility of any such proceeding, which, carried out between *sous-offi-ciers*, might form the basis of a French drama, but which was impossible of execution between English gentlemen, and elected absence from Squab-street, and total ignorance of Mr. Caird's mode of procedure, as his best aids to a tolerably quiet life for himself. Besides, absence from Squab-street meant absence from Madeleine; and absence from Madeleine meant a great deal to Ronald Kilsyth. He, in his self-examination found Ma-deleine's behaviour since her marriage the one point on which he could neither satisfy himself by a feeling of pity nor bluster himself into a fit of indignation. He knew well enough what her abstracted manner, her dulness, her sad weary preoccupied mind, her impossibility to join in the nonsensical talk floating around her,—he knew well enough what all these symptoms meant. If he had ever doubted that his sister had a strong affection for Wilmot—and it is due to his perspicacity to say that no such doubt ever crossed his mind—he would have been certain of it now. If he had ever hoped—and he had hoped very earnestly—that any girlish predilection which his sister might have entertained for Wilmot was merely girlish and evanescent, and would pass away with her marriage, he could not more effectually have blighted any such chance than by marrying her to the man whose suit he, her brother, had himself urged her to accept. Perhaps under happier circumstances that childish dream would have passed away, merged into a more happy realisation; but as it had eventuated, Ronald knew perfectly well that Madeleine could not but contrast the blank loveless present with the bright past, could not but compare the days when she now sat solitary and uncared for with those when the man for whom she had such intense veneration—for whom, as she doubtless had afterwards discovered, she had such honest, ear-

nest love—had given up everything else to attend
to her and shield her in the hour of danger. With
such feelings as these at his heart, it was but little
wonder that Ronald sedulously avoided being
thrown in Madeleine's way.

He had always been so " odd ;" his comings and
goings in Brook-street had been so uncertain; it
was so utterly impossible to tell when he might or
might not be expected at his father's house, that
his prolonged absence caused no astonishment to
any of the members of the family, nor to any one
of their regular visitors. Lady Muriel, indeed,
with a kind of guilty consciousness of participation
in his feelings, guessed the reason why her step-
son eschewed their society; but no one else. And
Lady Muriel, who from her first suspicion of
Ramsay Caird's conduct — suspicion not entertained, be it understood, until some time after the
marriage — had looked forward with great fear
and trembling to a grand *éclaircissement*, a search-
ing explanation with Ronald, in which she would
have to undergo an amount of cross-questioning
in his hardest manner, and a judgment which

would inevitably be pronounced against her, was rather glad that this whim had taken possession of Ronald, and that her *dies iræ* was consequently indefinitely deferred. But it happened one day that Ronald, walking down to Knightsbridge barracks, came upon his father waiting to cross the road at the corner of Sloane-street, and came upon him so " plump" and so suddenly, that retreat was impossible. The young man accordingly, seeing how matters stood, advanced, and took his father by the hand.

In an instant he saw that one other, at all events, had suffered from the—well, there was no other word for it—the disgrace, the discredit, to say the least of it, which had fallen on the family during the past few months. Kilsyth seemed aged by ten years. The light had died out of his bright blue eyes, and left them glassy and colourless, with red rims and heavy dark " pads" underneath each. The bright healthy colour had faded from his cheeks, and few would have recognised the lithe and active mountaineer, the never-tiring pedestrian, and the keen shot, in the bent and shrunken form which stood half-leaning on, half-idly dallying with, its stick. He pressed his son's hand warmly, however; and something like his well-known kind old smile lighted up his face as he exclaimed—

"Ronald, I'm glad to see you, my boy! very glad! You've not been near us for ages! And not merely that—I can understand that— we're not very good company for young people now in Brook-street; there's little inducement to come there now since poor Maddy has left us. But I don't think that I was ever half so long in London without dining with you as your guest over there at the barracks. I used to like an outing with your fellows there; it brisked me up, and made me forget what an old fogie I am growing; but—but you haven't given me the chance this time, sir,—you haven't given me the chance!"

There was something in the evidently strained attempt at cheeriness with which his father said these words which contrasted so strongly with the depression under which it was impossible for

him to prevent showing he was labouring, and
with the marked alteration in his personal appearance, that touched Ronald.deeply.   His heart
sank within him, and his tongue grew dry ; he
had to clear his throat before he replied — and
even then huskily—

"It *is* a long time since we've met, sir; and
I confess the fault is mine—entirely mine.   The
fact is I've been very much engaged lately—
regimental duty, and — and some business in
which I've been particularly interested—business
which I fear you would hardly care about —
and—"

"Likely enough, my dear boy!" said Kilsyth, coming to his rescue, as he floundered about
in a way very unusual to him.   "Likely enough!
I never did care particularly for a good many
of your pursuits, you know, Ronald, though I
tried very hard at one time—when you were
quite a lad, I recollect—to understand them and
share in them.   But that was not to be.   I was
not bright enough.   I'm of the old school, and
what we old fellows cared about seems to have

died out with our youth, and never to have
interested anybody ever since. I don't say this
complainingly — not in the least — but it was
deuced odd. However, I'm very glad I've met
you, Ronald, for I have long wished—and lately,
within the last few days more especially—to have
a talk with you, a serious talk, my boy, which
will take up some little time. Have you half-
an-hour you can give me now? I shall be very
glad if you have."

It was coming at last. He had but put off
the evil day, and now it was upon him. Well—
better to hear himself condemned by his father
than by anyone else. Let it come.

"My time is yours, sir," said Ronald, almost
echoing Wilmot, as he remembered, on the day
of that eventful interview in Charles-street. "I
shall of course be delighted to give my best attention to anything you may have to say."

"Well, then, let's take a turn in the Park
opposite," said Kilsyth, hooking his arm into his
son's. "Not among the people there, where we
should be perpetually interrupted by having to

speak to those folks who hail one so good-naturedly
at every step, but away on the grass there, by
ourselves."

The two men passed through the Albert Gate,
and turning to the right, struck on to the piece of
turf lying between the Row and the Drive.   A
few children were playing about, a few nurse-
maids were here and there gossiping together ;
else they had it all to themselves.

"I want to talk to you," commenced Kilsyth,
"about your sister—about Maddy.   I have been
a good deal to Squab-street in the last few weeks,
and I've thought Maddy looks anything but as
I should wish her to look.   Has that struck you,
Ronald ?"

"I—I'm sorry to say that I haven't seen
Madeleine for some little time, sir.   The business
which, as I just explained to you, has prevented
my coming to Brook-street has equally prevented
me from calling on her."

"Of course, yes! I beg pardon—I forgot!
Well, Maddy looks anything but well.   For a
long time past—indeed ever since her marriage

—she has been singularly low-spirited and dull; very unlike her usual self."

"I don't know that that is much to be wondered at. Madeleine was always a peculiar girl, in the sense that she had an extraordinary attachment for her home; and the fact of being parted from you, with whom all her life has been passed, and to whom she is devotedly attached, may explain the cause of any little temporary lowness of spirits."

"Ye-es, that's true so far; but it's not that; I wish I could think it was. What you say, though, Ronald, I think gets somewhat near the real cause. Maddy has been unlike most other girls of her class; much more home-y and domestic, thinking much more of those around her with whom she has been brought into daily contact than of the outside pleasures, if I may so call them. And she's had a great deal of love. She's accustomed to it, and can't get on without it. Love's just as essential to Madeleine as light to the flowers, or the keen clear air to the stags. She's had it all her life, and she would die without it. And, Ronald, I'll say to you what I'd not say to another soul upon earth, but what's lying heavy on my heart this month past—I doubt much whether she gets it, my boy; I doubt much whether she gets it."

The old man stopped suddenly in his walk, and clutched his son's arm, and looked up earnestly into his son's face. There was so much sharp agony in the glance, hurried and fleeting though it was, that Ronald scarcely knew what to say in reply to the quivering jerky speech.

His father saved him from his embarrassment by continuing : "I don't think she gets the love that she's been accustomed to, and that she had a right to expect. I tell you that Maddy is not happy, Ronald; that her little heart aches and pines for want of sympathy, for want of appreciation, for want of love. I'm an old fellow; but in this case I suppose my affection for my darling has opened my eyes, and I can see it all plainly."

" Don't you think, sir, that your undoubted devotion to Madeleine may, on the other hand, have had the effect of warping your judgment a little, and prejudicing you in the matter? Though I've not seen my sister very lately, when I did see her I confess I did not observe any marked difference in her—any difference at all from what she has been during the last few months."

"The last few months! That's just it; that's just what—however, we'll come to that presently. I *know* you're wrong, Ronald; I *know* that Madeleine is thoroughly changed and altered from the bright darling girl of the old days. And I know why, my boy! God help me, I know why!'

Again Ronald essayed to speak, and again he only muttered unintelligibly.

"Because her home is unhappy," said Kilsyth, stopping short in his walk, and dropping his voice to a whisper; "because the marriage into which she was—was persuaded—I will use no harsh words—has proved a wretched one for her; because her husband has proved himself to be— God forgive me—a scoundrel!"

"You speak strongly, sir, notwithstanding

your professions," said Ronald, on whom warm words of any kind had always the effect of rendering him even more cold and stoical than was his wont.

"I speak strongly because I feel strongly, Ronald! I don't expect you to share my feelings in this matter, but I do expect you to have some of your own, although you may not show them. For God's sake cast aside for a few minutes that cloak of frost in which you always shroud yourself, and let us talk as father and son about one who is daughter to the one and sister to the other!"

Ronald looked up in surprise. He had never seen his father so much excited before.

"I have no doubt about this," continued Kilsyth. "I have hoped against hope, and I have shut my eyes against what I have seen, hoping they might be fancies; and my ears against what I have heard, hoping they might be lies. But I can befool myself in this manner no longer. Ah! to think of my darling thus—to think of my darling thus!" Tears started to the old man's eyes, and he smote fiercely with his stick upon the ground.

" If you are really persuaded of this, sir," said Ronald, " it is our duty to take immediate measures. Mr. Caird must be taught—"

" Who brought him to our house?" asked Kilsyth in a storm of passion; " or rather—not that—but when he was brought, who backed him up and encouraged him in every way? You, Ronald ! you—you—you ! By your advice he was permitted free access to the house, was constantly thrown in Madeleine's company, and gave the world to understand that he was going to marry her. I postponed the settling of the engagement once; but the second time, when — when I fancied that the child might have had some other views—might have formed some other fancy—you persuaded me to agree, and—"

" You should apportion the blame properly, sir," said Ronald in his coldest tones. " I did not introduce Caird to your house, nor was I the principal advocate of his cause."

" You're quite right, Ronald, quite right—

and I've been hasty and passionate and inconside-
rate, I know ; but if you knew how utterly heartbroken I am—"

"I think, with regard to Mr. Caird," interrupted Ronald, " the best plan will be—"

" No, no; not Caird now—leave him for the
present; afterwards we'll do for him.   Now about
Maddy—nothing but about Maddy—and not about
her dulness, or anything of that kind, nor—worse,
much worse—you recollect—no, you didn't know ;
I think you weren't there—what Wilmot, Dr.
Wilmot, said to me at Kilsyth about her chest?
He told me that one of her lungs was threatened
—that the lungs were her weak point; and he
asked me whether any of our family had suffered
from such disease."

" Well, sir," said Ronald, anxiously now.

" This disease has been gaining ground for
months past; I'm sure of it.   I have had my
opinions for some time: but Maddy never complains, you know, and I didn't like to ask her
about her symptoms, lest she might be frightened.
But within the last few days she has been so bad

that it has been evident to us all, to myself and—
and Lady Muriel that the disease was on the increase. She caught cold at the theatre the other
night, and her cough is now frightful. I have
seen her just now, poor darling ! She was on the
sofa, but very weak—all they could do to get her
there—and when the paroxysms of coughing come
on it's awful to see her—she hardly seems to have
the strength to live through them. My poor darling Maddy !"

" What do the doctors say, sir? Who is
attending her ?"

" Whittaker — Dr. Whittaker — a very good
man in his way, I daresay, but—I don't know—
somehow I don't think much of him. Now that is
the very point I wanted to talk to you about. Somehow — how, I never understood — somebody — I
don't know who—offended Dr. Wilmot, a man to
whom we were under the greatest obligation for
kindness rendered ; and though he has been back
in England for some time, he has never called in
Brook-street, nor on Madeleine even, since his
return. There is no one in whom I have such

faith ; there is no one, I am convinced, who un-
derstands Madeleine's constitution like Wilmot :
and I want to know what is the best method for
us to put our pride in our pockets and implore
him to come and see her."

"You were not thinking of asking Dr. Wilmot to visit Madeleine ?"

"I was indeed.   What objection could there
possibly be ?"

"I suppose you know that he has retired from
practice, that he even declines to attend consultations, since he inherited Mr. Foljambe's money ?"

"I know that ; but I am perfectly certain,
from what I saw of him at Kilsyth, that if I were
to go to him and tell him the state of affairs, he
would overlook anything that may have annoyed
him, and come and see Maddy at once."

"That would be a condescension !" said Ronald.   "Perhaps it might be on the other side
that the ' overlooking' might be required.   However, there are other reasons, sir, why I, for one,
should think it highly inadvisable that Dr. Wilmot
should be requested to visit my sister."

"What are they, then, in Heaven's name, man?" said Kilsyth petulantly. "You don't seem to see that the matter is of the utmost urgency."

"It is because of its urgency that I speak of it at all; it is by no means a pleasant topic for me or for any of us. You spoke to me just now, sir, in warm words of the part I took in pressing Ramsay Caird to visit at your house, and supporting his claims for Madeleine. I don't know that I was at all eager for it at first; I'm certain I never cared particularly for Ramsay Caird; but I freely own that latterly I did my best for him, convinced that a speedy alliance with him was the only chance of rescuing Madeleine from another offer which I was sure was impending—which would have been far more objectionable, and yet which she would have accepted."

"Another offer?—from whom?"

"From the gentleman of whom you entertain so high an opinion—from Dr. Wilmot."

"From Wilmot! An offer from Wilmot to Madeleine! You must be mad, Ronald!"

" I never was more sane in my life, sir. I repeat, I am perfectly certain Dr. Wilmot was in love with Madeleine, that he would have made her an offer, and that she would have accepted him."

" And why should she not have accepted him? God knows I would have welcomed him for a son-in-law, and—"

" I scarcely think this is the time to enter into that subject, sir; but now that I have enlightened you, I presume you see the objection to calling in Dr. Wilmot to my sister."

" I see the difficulty, Ronald; but the objection and the difficulty shall be overcome. You shall yourself go and see Wilmot; and I know he'll not refuse you."

" Don't you think, sir, before I take upon myself to do that, it would be, to say the least of it, desirable that we should consult Madeleine's husband ?"

" Indeed I do not, Ronald," said Kilsyth; " indeed I do not. In giving up my daughter to Mr. Caird I yielded privileges which I alone had enjoyed from her birth, and which I would gladly have retained until her death or mine. But I did not give up the privilege of watching over her health, more especially when it has been so shamefully neglected; and I shall claim the power to use it now."

"And you think, after all I have told you, that there is no objection to asking Dr. Wilmot to visit Madeleine?"

"See here, Ronald!—I will be very frank with you in this matter—I think that if I had known all you have told me now seven or eight months ago, we should never have had this conversation. For I firmly believe that—granting your ideas were correct—if my darling had married Wilmot, he would have taken care both of her health and her happiness, both of which have been so grossly neglected."

The father and son took their way in silence back across the grass, each filled with his own reflections. They had only reached the Albert Gate, and were about to pass through it into the street, when a brougham passed them, and a gentleman sitting in it gravely saluted them.

"Good heavens!" exclaimed Kilsyth; "there's Wilmot!"

"Yes," said Ronald. He was surprised, and secretly agitated by the sight of the man towards whom his feelings had insensibly changed, and was hardly master of his emotion.

The carriage had passed on, but Kilsyth was standing still at the crossing.

"What an extraordinary chance—what a wonderful Providence, I should say!" said Kilsyth; "the only man I have confidence in—fancy his passing by just at this time! Thank God! No chance of his calling at Brook-street before he goes home, as he used to do; we must go on to his house at once and leave a message for him." Here the impetuous old gentleman hailed a hansom, which drew up abruptly in dangerous proximity to his toes.

"Stop a moment," said Ronald. "You had better get home, in case I can persuade Dr. Wilmot to call, and tell Lady Muriel; it will save time. I will go on to his house."

"All right," said Kilsyth in a voice of positive

cheerfulness. The mere sight of Wilmot had acted like a strong cordial upon him—had restored his strength and his confidence.

"Don't I recollect how he saved her before, when she was much worse, when she was actually in the clutch of a mortal disease? And he will save her again! he will save her again!" said the old man to himself as he drove homewards. He went directly to Lady Muriel's boudoir, and communicated to her the glad tidings of Ronald's mission, which had filled him with hope and joy.

The rich red colour flew to Lady Muriel' cheek, and the light shone in her dark eyes. To her too the news was precious, delicious; but not so the intelligence which formed its corollary. What! Ronald Kilsyth gone to solicit Dr. Wilmot's attendance on his sister! Ronald Kilsyth bringing about the renewal of this danger which she, apparently ably assisted by fate, had put far from her! What availed Wilmot's return, if he might see Madeleine again—might be with her? What availed it that Madeleine was no longer in the house with him, that she was free to see him,

to enjoy his society undisputed? As Kilsyth saw
how her face lighted up, how her colour rose, he
rejoiced in her sympathy with his feelings, with
his hope and relief, he blessed her in his heart for
her love for his Madeleine. And she listened to
him, dominated in turn by irresistible joy and by
burning anger.

CHAPTER VII.

TOO LATE.

THAT there can be such a thing as a broken heart; that love, misguided, misdirected, fixed upon the wrong object, and never finding "its earthly close," having to pine in secret, and to take out its revenge in saying deteriorating and spiteful things of its successful rival, ever kills, is nowadays generally accepted as nonsense. In the daily round of the work-a-day life there are too many things hourly cropping up to allow a man of any spirit to permit himself to hug to his bosom the corpse of a dead joy, or to bemoan over the reminiscence of vanished happiness. He must be up and doing; he must go in to his business, read his newspaper, give his orders to his clerks, write his letters—or at least sign them; go to his club, eat his dinner, and go through his ordinary

routine, each item of which fills up his time, and
prevents him from dwelling on the atrocious per-
fidy of the Being who has deceived him. The
evening has generally been considered a favour-
able time for indulging in those reflections which,
by their bitterness, bring about the anatomical
consequences so much to be deplored; but your
modern Strephon either forgets his own woes in
reading of the fictitious woes of others, duly supplied by Mr. Mudie, or in witnessing them de-
picted on the stage, or in listening to the cynical
wisdom of the smoking-room, which, if he duly
imbibe it, leads him rather to think he has had
a wonderful escape; or in the friendly game of
whist, when deference to his partner's interest, to
say the least of it, requires that he should keep
his thoughts from wandering into that subject so
redolent of bitter-sweet. The heart-breaking business is out of date, it is *rococo*, it is bygone; and
one might as well look to see the brazen greaves
of bold Sir Lancelot flashing in our English imi-
tation of the sunshine, and to hear the knight sing-
ing "Lirra-lirra!" as he rode up the banks of

the Serpentine, as to believe in its existence now-adays.

So that those who may have imagined that Chudleigh Wilmot had given up all relish of and interest in life must have been grievously disappointed. When he first went abroad, grief and rage were in his heart, and he cared but little what became of him. When he first received the news of Mr. Foljambe's bequest, there sprung up in him a new feeling of hope and joy, such as he had never had before, which lasted but a very few hours, being uprooted and cast out by the announcement of Madeleine's marriage in the newspaper. When he returned to London, his mind was so far made up, that he contemplated very calmly the possibility of such an existence—without Madeleine, that is to say — as a few hours previously he had deemed impossible; and though on first entering on the new life the old ghosts which "come to trouble joy" would occasionally await him; and though after that chance meeting with Madeleine and Lady Muriel in the Park he was for some little time much disturbed, yet, on the whole, he managed to live his life quietly, soberly, peacefully, and not unhappily.

The man who, after years of active employment, inherits or obtains a competency, and straightway lies upon his oars and looks round him for the remainder of his life, immediately falls into a sad way, and comes speedily to a bad end. Wilmot was quite sufficient man of the world to be aware of this; and though he had retired from the active practice of his profession, indeed from practising in any way, he still kept up his medical studies, and now became one of the most sought-after and most influential contributors to the best of our scientific publications. In this way he found exercise enough for his mental faculties, which had been somewhat burdened and overtasked with all the hard work which he had gone through in his early life; and as for the rest, he found he had done society a great injustice in estimating its resources so meanly as he had been used to do. By degrees he gave up the rule which he had at first kept so strictly, never to go into ladies' society; and the first plunge made he felt that he

enjoyed himself therein more than in any other.
He found that his reputation, which had been considerably increased by the literary work on which
he had recently engaged, smoothed the way for
him on first introduction; and that the fact of
his being a middle-aged widower secured for him
that pleasant license accorded to fogies, of which
only fogies are thoroughly conscious and appre-
ciative. Instead of losing caste or position, he felt
that he had gained it; all the best people who had
been his patients in the old days kept up their
acquaintance with him, and asked him to their
houses; and after the publication of a paper by
him on a momentous subject of the day, containing new and striking views which at once com-
manded public attention and attracted public
comment, he was placed on a Royal Commission
among some of the first men of the time, and an
intimation was conveyed to him that Government
would be glad to avail themselves of his services.

And the old wearing, tearing feeling of love
and disappointment and regret which had blighted
so many hours of his life, and which he thought

at one time would sap life itself, was gone, was it?
Well, not entirely.   It had been an era in his life
which was never to be forgotten, which was never
to be otherwise renewed.   Night after night he
saw pretty charming girls, all of whom would have
been pleased by a flattering word from the cele-
brated Dr. Wilmot, many of whom would have
listened more than complacently to anything he
might have chosen to say to them,—" he is very
rich, my dear, and goes into excellent society."
But he never said anything, because he never
thought anything of the kind.   Sometimes when
alone, in the pauses of his work, he would look up
from off his book or his paper, and then straightway he would see—although his thoughts had been
previously engrossed with something entirely different—a bright flushed face, with blue eyes, and a
nimbus of golden hair surrounding it.   But for a
moment he would see it, and then it would fade
away; but in that moment how many memories
had it evoked!   Sometimes he would take from
a special drawer in his desk a small knot of blue
ribbon, and a thin letter, frayed in its folds, and

bearing traces of having been for some time carried in the pocket.   Slight memorials these of the
only love of a lifetime which had now extended
to some forty years ; not much to show in return
for an all-absorbing passion which at one time
threatened to have dire effect on his health, on his
life—yet cherished all the more, perhaps, on account of their insignificance ! These were memorials of Miss Kilsyth, be it understood : of Mrs.
Ramsay Caird Chudleigh always rigidly repeated
to himself that he knew nothing—that he never
would know anything.

But one morning Chudleigh Wilmot was sitting
in his library after his breakfast, his slippered
feet resting idly on a chair, he himself in placid
enjoyment of the newspaper and a cigar, which,
since he had freed himself from professional restraint, he had taken as a pleasant solace, when
suddenly, and without being in any way led up
to, the subject of his dream of the previous night
flashed suddenly across his mind. It was about
Madeleine.   He remembered that he had seen her
lying outstretched on her bed dead ; there were

Christmas berries in her golden hair, and the robe which covered her was embroidered with the initial letters of his name twisted into a monogram, such as was engraved on the binding of a present of books which he had recently received from one of his great friends, and on the little finger of her hand, which lay outside the coverlet, was Mabel's signet-ring. He remembered all this vividly now; remembered too how, when he had gone forward with the intention of taking off the ring, a female form, clad in dark sweeping garments, but with its face shrouded, had risen by the bedside and motioned him away. He remembered how he felt persuaded, although the face was hidden, that the form was known to him—was that of Henrietta Prendergast; how he had persisted in approaching; and how at length the muffled form had spoken, saying only these words, "It was not to be!" What followed he could not remember: there was a kind of chaos, out of which rose figures of Whittaker and Colonel Jefferson, the man whom he had met in Scotland, and Ronald Kilsyth in full uniform, with his sword drawn and pointed at his

(Chudleigh's) heart; and then he had waked, and the whole remembrance of the dream had departed from him until that moment, when simultaneously the door of his room was thrown open, and Ronald Kilsyth stood before him.

That was no dream. Wilmot thought at first that his waking fancies were running in the track of his sleeping thoughts; but there was Ronald Kilsyth, somewhat changed from the man he remembered—less grim and stoical, a trifle less cynical, and a trifle more human,—but still Ronald Kilsyth standing before him.

"You are surprised to see me, Dr. Wilmot," said Ronald, advancing hesitatingly,—" surprised to see me here, after — after so long an interval."

"On the last occasion of our meeting, Captain Kilsyth," replied Wilmot, " you were good enough to tell me that you objected to the ordinary set phrases of society, and preferred straightforward answers. I have not forgotten that interview, or anything that passed therein; and I have every desire, believe me, to accommodate you—at least so far as that wish is concerned. My straightforward answer to your question is, I *am* surprised to see you in this house."

"I looked for no other reply. You seem to forget that, even so far ago as our last meeting, you were pleased to fall in with my whim, and to answer me with perfect candour, however painful it might have been—it was—to you. That conversation will doubtless be remembered by you, Dr. Wilmot."

What did this mean? Was the man come here, in the assurance of his own cold, calm stoicism, to triumph over him? Whence this most indecorous outrage on his privacy, this insult to his feelings? Of all men, this man knew how he had suffered, and how he had borne his sufferings. Why, then, was he here, at such a moment, with such words on his lips?

"I perfectly remember that conversation, Captain Kilsyth," was all Wilmot replied.

"You will spare me, then, a great deal of acute pain in referring to it," said Ronald. "Refer to

it I must, but my reference will be of the most
general kind. I sought that interview beseech-
ing you"—Wilmot gave a short half-laugh, which
Ronald noticed—" Well, you stickle for terms,
it appears,—demanding of you to give up a pursuit in which you were then engaged—a pursuit
to which you attached the greatest interest, but
which I knew would not only be futile in its
results to you, but would be fraught with distress
and danger to one who was very dear to me.
You acquiesced in my reasoning—at great sorrow
and disappointment to yourself, I know—and you
gave up the pursuit."

" You are very good to make such large
allowances for me, Captain Kilsyth," said Wilmot in a hard dry voice. " Yes, I gave it up;
at great sorrow and disappointment to myself,
as you are good enough to say."

" I can fully understand the feelings which
now influence you, Dr. Wilmot," said Ronald,
far more gently than was his wont; " and, believe me, I do not quarrel with or take exception
at the tone in which they are now expressed.

You gave up that pursuit, and you carried out the intention you then expressed to me of leaving England."

"I did. I left England within a fortnight of that conversation. I should not have returned when I did—I should not have returned even now, most probably—had it not been for circumstances then utterly unforeseen, but of which you may have heard, which compelled me to come back at once."

Ronald bowed; he had heard of those circumstances, he said.

"And now, pardon me, Captain Kilsyth, if I just run through what has occurred. It cannot be, you will allow, less unpleasant for me to do so than for you; but since we have met again,—at an interview not of my seeking, recollect,—it is as well that they should be understood. You told me in my consulting-room in Charles-street that you had reason to believe that your sister, Miss Kilsyth, was—let us put it plainly—loved by me. You said that, or at least you implied that, you had reason to believe that she was

interested in me. You told me that any question
of marriage between us was impossible; first,
because I had originally made your sister's acquaintance when I was a married man; secondly,
because my station in life—you put it kindly, as
a gentleman would, but that was the gist of your
argument—because my station in life was inferior
to hers. I do not know, Captain Kilsyth," continued Wilmot, whose voice grew harder as he
proceeded, "that your reasoning was so subtle
in either case as not to admit of controversy, perhaps even of disproof; but I felt that when a
young lady's name was in question, when there
was, as you assured me there was—and you were
much more a man of the world than I—the
chance of the slightest slur being cast on her, it
was my duty to sacrifice my own feelings, however strong they might have been in the matter.
I did so. To the best of my ability I stamped
out my love; I pocketed my pride; I gave up
the best feelings of my nature, and I did as you
and your friends wished. I went abroad, and remained grizzling and feeding on my own heart

for months. At length I heard of a stroke of good
fortune which had befallen me. I had previously
made for myself a name which was respected
and honoured; and you, who know more of these
things than your compeers, or people in your
'set,' can appreciate the worth of the renown
which a man makes off his own bat by the exercise of his talents; and by the chance which I
have named I had now inherited a fortune — a
large fortune for any man not born to wealth.
When this news reached me, my first thought
was, Now, surely, my coast is clear. I can go
back to England ; I can say to Miss Kilsyth's
friends, I am renowned; I am rich; I am, I hope,
a gentleman in the ordinary acceptation of the
term. If this young lady will accept my court,
why should it not be paid her ? Within twenty-
four hours of my learning of my inheritance, of
my determination, I heard that Miss Kilsyth was
married."

"There was no stipulation, I believe, Dr.
Wilmot—at least so far as I am concerned—no
compact, no given time during which Miss Kilsyth

should keep single, in the view of anything that might happen to you ?"

"None in the world; and so far as Miss Kilsyth is concerned—her name is being bandied between us in the course of conversation, but it is my duty to say that I have not the smallest atom of complaint to make against her. To this hour, so far as I know, she is unacquainted with my feelings towards her, and can consequently be held responsible for no acts of hers at which I may feel aggrieved. But you must let me continue. I will not tell you what effect the intelligence of Miss Kilsyth's marriage had on me. I had been raised to the highest pinnacle of hope, I was cast down into the lowest depths of despair. That concerned no one but myself. I returned to England. Miss Kilsyth was Mrs. Ramsay Caird —I had learned that from the public prints—no private announcement, no wedding-cards awaited me. The story of my vast inheritance got wind, as such things do, and all my friends—all my acquaintance, let me say, to use a more fitting word, called on me or sent their congratulations. From

your family, from Mrs. Ramsay Caird, I had not
the slightest notice.   The young lady whose life—
if you credit her father—I had saved a few months
previously, and her family, who professed themselves so grateful, ignored my existence.   To this
hour I have had no communication with Kilsyth,
with Lady Muriel, with the Ramsay Cairds.   I
met Lady Muriel and her daughter once by the
merest accident—an accident entirely unsought by
me—and they bowed to me as though I were a
tradesman who had been pestering for his bill.
What am I to gather from this treatment?   One
of two things—either that I was regarded merely
as the 'doctor' who was called in when his services were needed, but who, when he had fulfilled his functions and saved the patient, was no
more to be recognised than the butcher when he
had supplied the required joint of meat; or that,
by those who knew, or thought they knew, the
inner circumstances of the case, my moral character was so highly esteemed that, guessing I had
been in love with Miss Kilsyth, it was judged ex-
pedient that I should have no opportunity of ac-

quaintance with Mrs. Ramsay Caird. I ask you, Captain Kilsyth, which of these suppositions is correct?"

Wilmot spoke with great warmth. Ronald Kilsyth looked on with wonder; he could scarcely imagine that the man who now stood erect before him with flashing eye and curled lips, every one of whose sentences rang with scorn, was the same being who, on the occasion of their last interview, had urged his suit so humbly, and accepted his dismissal with such resignation.

After a short pause Ronald said: "You speak strongly, Dr. Wilmot, very strongly; but you have great cause for annoyance; and the fact that you have borne it so long in silence of course adds to the violence of your expressions now. I think I could soften your opinion—I think I could show that my father and Lady Muriel have had some excuse for their conduct; at all events, that they believed they were doing rightly in acting as they did. But this is not the time for me to enter into that discussion. I have come to you in the discharge of a mission which is urgent and

imperative.   You know me to be a cold and
a proud man, Dr. Wilmot, and will therefore
allow I must be convinced of its urgency when
I consented to undertake it.   I have come to say
to you—leaving all things for the present unex-
plained, and even in the state in which you have
just described them—I have come to say to you
my sister is very ill; will you go and see her?"
He was standing close by Wilmot as he spoke,
and saw him change colour, and reel as though
he would have fallen.

"Very ill?" he said, after a moment's pause,
with white lips and trembling voice.   "Mad—
Mrs. Caird, very ill?"

"Very ill; so ill, that my father is seriously
alarmed about her; so ill, that I have obeyed his
wishes, and ask you to come to her."

Wilmot was silent for a moment, in thought;
not that he had the smallest doubt as to what he
should do; but the news had come so suddenly
upon him, that he could scarcely comprehend its
significance.   Then he said, "Where is she? in
town?"

"She is—at her own house. I know I am asking you a great deal in begging you to go there, but—you won't refuse us, Wilmot?"

"I will go at once to your sister, Captain Kilsyth," said Wilmot, pressing Ronald's outstretched hand; "and God grant I may be of service to her!"

"I won't say any thanks; but you know how grateful we shall all of us be. Perhaps Madeleine had better be a little prepared for your visit; if you were to meet quite unexpectedly, it might agitate her."

Wilmot agreed in this, and promised to come that afternoon.

It was three o'clock—just the hour when Squab-street woke up, and became alive to the fact that day had dawned. The light had indeed penetrated the little street at its usual hour, and the sun had shone; but still Squab-street could not be considered to be fully awake. Tradesmen had come and gone; area-bells had rung out shrilly; grooms on horseback had fol-

lowed the Amazon daughters of the natives to
the morning-ride in the Row; governesses had
arrived, and had taken their young charges into
the neighbouring square garden for bodily exercise and mental recreation; neat little broughams
had deposited neat little foreigners, whose admis-
sion into the houses had been immediately followed by the thumping of the piano and the
screaming of the female voice; but the cream of
Squab-street society had not yet been seen, save
by its female attendants.   Three o'clock, however,
had arrived; luncheon was over, carriages began
to rattle up and down, the street resounded with
double knocks indefinitely prolonged, and all
the little passages were redolent of hair-powder.
All society's mummers were acting away at their
hardest; and all who passed up and down Squab-
street were too much engrossed with themselves
or their fellow-performers to notice a very blank
and mournful face looking out at them from the
drawing-room window of the little house at the
corner of the mews. This was Kilsyth's face,
which had been planted against the window for

the previous half-hour, in anxious expectation of Wilmot's arrival. Sick at heart, and overpowered by anxiety, the old man had taken his position where he could catch the first glimpse of him on whom his life now solely rested; and he scanned every vehicle that approached with eager eyes. At length a brougham, very different from that in which he used to pay his visits in his professional days, perfectly appointed, and drawn by horses which even Clement Penruddock himself could not have designated as "screws," drew up at the door, and Wilmot jumped out. Two minutes afterwards Kilsyth, with his eyes full of tears, was holding both his friend's hands, and murmuring to him his thanks.

"I knew you would come!" he said; "I knew you would come! No matter what had happened in the interval—no matter that, as they told me, you had retired from practice and went nowhere—I said, 'Let him know that Madeleine is very ill, and he'll come! he'll be sure to come!'"

"And you said right, my dear sir," said Wilmot, returning the friendly pressure; "and I only hope to Heaven that my coming now may be as efficacious as it was when you summoned me to Kilsyth—ah, how long ago that seems! Now tell me—for my conversation with Captain Kilsyth was necessarily brief, and admitted of no details concerning the state of his sister—the tendency to weakness on the lungs, which I spoke to you about just before I left Scotland, has increased, I fear?"

"It has been increasing rapidly, we fancy, for the last few months; and she is now never free from a cough, a hollow, dreadful cough, the paroxysms of which are sometimes terrible, and leave her perfectly exhausted. She never complains; on the contrary, she makes light of it, and struggles to hide her pain and weakness from us. But I fear she is very, very ill!" The old man's voice sunk as he said this, and the tears flowed down his cheeks.

"Come, come, you must not give way, my good friend; while there's life there's hope, you know; and what is very dreadful and hopeless to an unprofessional eye has a very different aspect frequently to those who have studied these diseases. I think Captain Kilsyth came here to prepare Mrs. Caird for my visit?"

"O yes, she expects you. She was greatly excited at first; so much so that we were afraid she would do herself harm; but I think she is calmer now."

"Then perhaps I had better go to her at once. It is always desirable in these cases as much as possible to avoid suspense. Will you show me the way?"

They went upstairs together; and when they arrived at the room, Kilsyth opened the door, and left Wilmot to enter by himself. As the door closed behind him, he looked up, and saw the woman whom he had loved with such devotion and yet with such bitter regret. She was lying on a sofa drawn across the window, propped up by pillows. She turned round at the noise of his entrance; and as soon as she recognised her visitor, her cheeks flushed to the deepest crimson. Wilmot advanced rapidly, with as cheerful a smile as he could assume, and took her hand—

her hot, wasted, and trembling hand—within both of his. She was dreadfully changed—he saw that in an instant. There were deep hollows in her cheeks, and round her blue eyes, which were now feverishly bright and lustrous, there were large bistre circles. She wore a white dressing-gown trimmed with blue,—such a one as was associated with his earliest recollections of her; and as he saw her lying back and looking up at him with earnest trusting gaze, he was reminded of the first time he saw her in the fever at Kilsyth, but with O what a difference in his hope of saving her!

"You see I have come back to you, Mrs. Caird," said Wilmot, seating himself by the sofa, but still retaining her hand. "You thought you had got rid of me for ever; but I am like the bottle-imp in the story, impossible to be sent away. Now, own you are surprised to see me!"

"I am not indeed, Dr. Wilmot," Madeleine replied, in a voice the hollow tones of which went to Wilmot's heart. Ah, how unlike the sweet,

clear, ringing tones which he so well remembered!
"I am not indeed surprised to see you. I had a
perfect conviction," she said very calmly, "that
I should see you once again. At that time—at
Kilsyth, you remember—I thought I was going
to die, you know; and when I knew I should
recover, as I lay in a dreamy half-conscious state,
I recollect having a presentiment that when I did
die you would be near me—that you would stand
by my bedside, as you used to do, and—"

"My dearest Mrs. Caird, I cannot listen to
you; my—my child, for God's sake don't talk in
that way! I used to have to tell you to calm
yourself, you know; but now you must rouse up
—you must indeed."

"O no, Dr. Wilmot; not rouse myself to any
action, not wake up again to the dreary struggle
of life! O no; let me sink quietly into my grave,
but—"

His hand trembled with emotion as he laid his
finger lightly on her lip, and his voice was choked
and husky as he said: "I must insist! You used

to obey me implicitly, you recollect; and you must show that you have not forgotten your old ways. And now tell me all about yourself."

Half an hour afterwards, as Wilmot was descending the stairs, he met Kilsyth at the drawing-room door, with haggard looks and trembling hands, waiting for him. They went into the drawing-room together; and the old man, carefully closing the door behind him, turned to his friend, and said in broken accents: "Well, what do you say? what—what do you think?"

Wilmot's face was very grave, graver than Kilsyth had ever seen it, even at the worst time of the fever, as he said: "I think it is a very serious case, my dear friend—a very serious case."

"Has the—the mischief increased much since you detected it—up in Scotland?"

"The disease has spread very rapidly—very rapidly indeed."

"And you — you think that she is — in danger?"

"I think—it would be useless, it would be

unmanly in me to withhold the truth from you;
I fear that Mrs. Caird's state is imminently dangerous, and that—"

Wilmot stopped, for Kilsyth reeled and almost
fell. Recovering himself after a moment, he said,
in a low hoarse whisper: " Change of climate—
Madeira—Egypt—anywhere ?"

" No; she has not sufficient strength to bear
the journey. If she had spent last winter at
Cannes, and had gone on in the spring to Egypt—
but it is too late."

" Too late !" shrieked Kilsyth, bursting into an
agony of grief; " too late ! My darling child ! my
darling, darling child !"

" My poor friend," said Wilmot, himself deeply
affected, " what can I say to comfort you in this
awful trial? what can I do ?"

" One thing !" said the old man, rising from
the sofa on which he had thrown himself, " there is
one thing you can do—visit her, watch her, attend
her ; you'll see her again, won't you, Wilmot ?"

" Constantly—and to the end. She knows

that. I made her that promise just now;" and he wrung his friend's hand and left him.

" Dr. Wilmot, I believe? Will you oblige me by two minutes' conversation? You don't remember me? I am Mr. Caird. In this room, if you please."

Wilmot, thus inducted into the dining-room, bowed, and took the chair pointed out to him. He had not recognised Mr. Caird at the first glance in the dim little passage ; but he knew him again now, albeit Mr. Caird's style of dress and general bearing were very different from what they had been in the old days. Mr. Caird had just come in, and brought a great quantity of tobacco-smoke in with him ; and a decanter of brandy, an empty soda-water bottle, and a fizzing tumbler, were on the table before him.

" I beg your pardon for troubling you, Dr. Wilmot; but I didn't know you were expected, or I should of course have been here to meet you. The people in Brook-street manage all these matters in—well, to say the least of it, in a curious way. You have seen Mrs. Caird—what is your opinion of her ?"

What Wilmot knew of this man was that he was courteous, gentlemanly, and good-tempered— all in his favour. He had heard the rumours current in society about Caird, but they had passed unheeded by him; men of Wilmot's calibre pay little attention to rumours. So he said, "Do you wish me to tell you my real opinion, Mr. Caird ?"

"Your real, candid opinion."

Then Wilmot repeated what he had said to Kilsyth.

The young man looked at him earnestly for a moment; shook his head as though he had been struck a sudden, stunning blow; then muttered involuntarily, as it were, "Poor Maddy !"

Wilmot rose to go, but Caird stopped him.

"One question more, Dr. Wilmot—how long may—may the end be deferred ?"

"I should fear not more than a few—three or four—months."

When Wilmot was gone, Ramsay Caird, having lit a fresh cigar, said " Poor Maddy!" again ; but this time he added, " since it was to be, it will be, about the time ;" and for the next hour he occupied himself with arithmetical calculations in his pocket-book.

CHAPTER VIII.

QUAND MEME!

In years to come it was destined to be a marvel to Wilmot how he lived through the days and the weeks of that time. If they had not been so entirely filled with supreme suffering, with despairing effort—if there had been any interval, any relaxation from the immense task imposed upon him, he might have broken down under it. He might have said, " I will not stay here, and see this woman whom I love die in her youth, in her beauty, in the very springtide of her life. I will go away. I will not see it, at least; I who have not the right to shut out all others, and gather up the last days of her life into a treasury of remembrance, in which no other shall have a share. No man is called upon to suffer that which he can avoid. I will go!" But there was no time

for Wilmot, no chance for him to reach such a
conclusion, to take this supreme resolution of despair.   The whole weight of the family trouble
was thrown upon him; and he, in comparison with
whose grief that of all the others, except Kilsyth's,
was insignificant, was the one to whom all looked
for support and hope.   As for Ramsay Caird, he
adopted the easy and plausible *rôle* of a sanguine
man.   He had the greatest possible respect for
Dr. Wilmot's opinion, the utmost confidence in
his ability; but the doctor's talent gave him the
very best grounds for security.   He was quite
sure Wilmot would set Madeleine all right.   She
had youth on her side—and only just think how
Wilmot had "pulled her through" at Kilsyth!
And as nobody occupied themselves particularly
with what Ramsay thought, he was permitted to
indulge his incorrigible *insouciance*, and to render
to Dr. Wilmot's talent the original homage of
believing it superior to his judgment and his
avowed conviction.   For the rest, Ramsay professed himself, and with reason, to be the
worst person in the world in a sick-room—

no use, and "awfully frightened;" and accordingly he seldom made his appearance in Madeleine's room, after the daily visit of a few minutes, which was *de rigueur*, and during which he invariably received the same answer to his inquiries, that she was better—a statement which it suited him to receive as valid, and which he therefore did so receive. Wilmot saw very little of him; no part of the hardness of his task came to him from Madeleine's husband. It was at her father's hands that Wilmot suffered most, and most constantly. Kilsyth held two articles of faith in connection with Wilmot: the first, that he was infallible in judgment; the second, that he was inexhaustible in skill and resources. And now these articles of belief clashed, and Kilsyth was swayed about between them,—a prey now to helpless grief, again to groundless and unreasonable hope. Certainly Madeleine was very ill. Wilmot was right, no doubt; but then Wilmot would save her: he had saved her before, when she was also very ill. Then the poor father would have the difference between fever and consumption, in point of assured fatality, forced upon his attention, and an interval of despair would set in. But whether his mood was hope or despair, an effort to attain resignation, or a mere stupor of fear and grief, Wilmot had to witness, Wilmot had to combat them all. The old man clung to the doctor with piteous eagerness and tenacity on his way to begin the watch over his patient which he maintained daily for hours, as he had done in the old time at Kilsyth—time in reality so lately past, but seeming like an entire lifetime ago. When he left her to take the short and troubled sleep which fell upon her in the afternoon; in the evening, when he came again; at night, after he had administered the medicine which was to procure her a temporary reprieve from the cough, which her father could no longer endure to hear, Kilsyth would waylay him, beset him with questions, with entreaties — or, worse still, look speechless into his face with imploring haggard eyes.

This to the man for whom the young life ebbing away, with terrific rapidity indeed, but with merciful ease on the whole, was the one treasure held by the earth, so rich for others, such a wilderness for him! Yes — her life! When he knew she was married, and thus parted from him for ever, he had thought the worst that could have come to him had come. But from the moment he had looked again into the innocent sweet blue eyes, and read, with the unerring glance of the practised physician, that death was looking out at him from them, he learned his error. Then too he learned how much, and with what manner of love, he loved Madeleine Kilsyth.

"Give her life, and not death, O gracious Disposer of both! and I am satisfied—and I am happy! Life, though I never see her face again; life, though she never hears my name spoken, or remembers me in her lightest thought; life, though it be to bless her husband, and to transmit her name to his children; life, though mine be wasted at the ends of the earth!" This was the cry of his soul, the utterance of the strong man's anguish. But he knew it was not to be; the physician's eye had been unerring indeed.

Lady Muriel bore herself on this, as on every

other occasion, irreproachably. The first enun-
ciation of the doctor's opinion had startled her.
She did not love her step-daughter, but of late she
had been on more affectionate terms with her ; and
it was not possible that she could learn that she
was doomed to an early death without terror and
grief. Lady Muriel knew well how unspeakably
dear to Kilsyth his daughter was; and apart from
her keen womanly sympathies all enlisted for the
fair young sufferer, she felt with agonising acute-
ness for her husband's suffering. The first meeting between Lady Muriel and Wilmot had been
under agitating circumstances; and the appeal
made to him by Kilsyth had at once established
him on the old footing with them — a footing
which had not existed previously in London, having
been interrupted by Wilmot's domestic affliction,
and the tacit but resolute opposition of Ronald.
But even then, in that first interview, when emotion was permissible, when Dr. Wilmot was forced
by his position to make a communication to the
father and brother which even a stranger must
necessarily have found painful, and though he im-

posed superhuman control over his feelings, Lady Muriel had seen the truth, or as much of the truth as one human being can ever see of the verities of the heart of another. She had received him gravely, but so that, had he cared to interpret her manner, it might have told him he was welcome in more than the sense of his value in this dread emergency; and it had been a sensible relief to Ronald to perceive that Lady Muriel had not suffered the pride and suspicion which had dictated her remonstrance to him to appear in any word or look of hers which Wilmot could perceive. But when Lady Muriel was alone she said to herself bitterly:

"He did love her, then; he does love her! He is awfully changed; and this has changed him—to her illness, not the fear of her death—the change is the work of months—but the loss of her. Her marriage—this has made his life valueless, this has made him what he is." Then she remained for a long time sunk in thought, her dark eyes shaded by her hand. At length she said, half aloud,

" She is not all to be pitied, even if this be indeed true and past remedy. She has been well beloved."

There was a whole history of solitude and vain aspiration in the words. Had not she too, Lady Muriel Kilsyth, been well beloved? True; but all the homage, all the devotion of an inferior nature could not satisfy hers. This woman would be content only with the love of a man her intellectual superior, her master in strength of purpose and of will. She had seen him; he had come; and he loved not her, but the simple girl with blue eyes and golden hair who was dying, and whom he would love faithfully when she should be dead. Lady Muriel did not deceive herself. She had the perfect comprehension of Wilmot which occult sympathy gives—she knew that he would never love another woman. She knew, when she recalled the ineffable mournfulness which sat upon his face, not the garment of an occasion, but the habitual expression which it had taken, that the hope which but for her might have been realised, had been the forlorn hope of

his life. It was over now; and he was beaten by
fate, by death, by Lady Muriel's will. He would
lay down his arms; he would never struggle again.

Knowing this, Lady Muriel Kilsyth dreamed
no more. The vision of a love which, pure and
blameless, would have elevated, fortified, and
sweetened her life, faded never to return. Her
gentle step-daughter, who would have been inca-
pable of such a thought or such a wish, had
she known how Lady Muriel had acted towards
her, was at that moment amply avenged.

In vain she had laboured to effect this loveless marriage; in vain she had placed in the un-
trustworthy hands of Ramsay Caird the happiness
and the fortune of her husband's beloved daughter; in vain had she been deaf to the truer, better
promptings of her conscience, to the haunting
thought of the responsibility which she had undertaken towards the girl, to the remembrance of
Madeleine's dead mother, which sometimes came
to her and troubled her sorely; in vain had
she tempted that dread and inexorable law of
retribution, which might fall upon the heads of

her own children.   How mad, how guilty, she
had been!   She saw it all now; she understood
it all now.   How could she, who had learned to
comprehend, to appreciate Wilmot,—how could
she have imagined for a moment that any senti-
ment once really entertained by him could be
light and passing!   She recognised, with respect
at least, if with an abiding sense of humiliation,
the truth, the strength, the eternal duration of
Wilmot's love for Madeleine.   Truly, many things,
in addition to the beautiful young form, were destined to go down into the grave of Madeleine
Kilsyth.

There was so much similarity between the
thoughts of Lady Muriel and those of Chudleigh
Wilmot, that he too, after that first visit, which
had shown him the dying girl and revealed to
him how he loved her, pondered also upon an
unconscious vengeance fulfilled.

Mabel! She had died in his absence, neglected by him, inflicting upon him an agonising
doubt, almost a certainty, but at least a doubt
never to be resolved in this world—a dread never

to be set at rest. He did not believe that had he been with her he could have saved her; but no matter: he had stayed away; he had given to another the love, the care, the time, the skill that should have been hers, that were her right by every law human and divine. And now! The woman he had preferred to her, the woman by whose side he had lingered, the woman he loved, was dying, and he had come to her aid too late! He could see her, it was true; he might be with her; it was possible he might hear her last words—might see her draw her last breath; but she was lost to him, lost unwon, lost for ever, as Mabel had been! It was late in the night before Wilmot had sufficiently mastered these thoughts and the emotions which they aroused to be able to apply himself to studying the details of Madeleine's case, and arranging his plan, not indeed of cure, but of alleviation.

Among the letters awaiting his attention there was one from Mrs. Prendergast. She requested him to call on her; she wished to consult him concerning the matter they had talked of. The

following morning he wrote her a line saying he
could not attend to anything for the present; and
subsequently Henrietta learned from Mrs. Charlton, through Mrs. M'Diarmid, that Wilmot had
consented to act as physician to Mrs. Caird, whom
he pronounced to be in hopeless consumption.

Henrietta went home grave and pensive,
thinking much of her dead friend, Mabel Wilmot.

Time had gone inexorably on since that day,
laden every hour of it with grief to Wilmot, with
immense and complicated responsibility, with the
dread of the rapidly-approaching end. There had
been hours—no, not hours, moments—when he
almost persuaded himself that he might be wrong,
that it was still time, that a warm climate might
yet avail. But the delusion was only momentary;
and he had told Madeleine's father and brother
from the first that she was unfit for a journey, that
the most merciful course was to let her die at
home in peace, among the people and the things
to whom and to which she was accustomed. He
understood the attachment of an invalid to the

inanimate objects around her; an attachment strongly developed in Madeleine, whose dressing-room, where she lay on the sofa all day, contained all her girlish treasures. She was always awake early in the morning, and anxious to be carried from her bed to her sofa, whence she would wist-fully watch the door until it opened and admitted Wilmot. Then she would smile—such a happy smile too! Only a pale reflection in point of brightness, it is true, of the radiant smile of the past, but full of the old trust and happiness and peace. Her father came early too, and received the report of how she had passed the night, and controlled himself wonderfully, poor old man! for agitation and disquiet were very bad for his dar-ling; and he was strengthened by Wilmot's ex-ample. It never occurred to Kilsyth to remember that Wilmot was "only the doctor," and therefore might well be calm; he never reasoned about Wilmot at all—he only felt and trusted. The world outside the sick-room went on as usual. Within it Madeleine Caird lay dying, not poeti-cally, not of the fanciful extinction which consumption becomes in the hands of the poet and the romancer, but of the genuine, veritable, terrible disease, not to be robbed by wealth, or even by comfort or skill, of its terrors. Those who know what is meant when a person is said to be dying of consumption need no amplification of the awful significance of the phrase. Those who do not—may they remain in their ignorance!

And Madeleine? Amid the contending emotions, amid the varied suffering which surrounded her, and had all its origin in her, how was it with Madeleine? On the whole, it was well. A strange phrase to apply to a young woman, a young wife, an idolised daughter, who was dying thus, of a disease which kills more thoroughly, so to speak, than any other, doing its dread office with slowness, and marking its progress day by day. She knew she was dying, though sometimes she did not feel it very keenly; the idea did not come to her as relating to herself, but with a sort of outside meaning. This dulness would last for days, and then she would be struck by the truth again, and would realise it with all the strength of

mind and body left to her. Realise it, not to be
terrified by it, not to resist it, not to appeal against
it, but to accept it, to acquiesce in it, to be satisfied and profoundly quiet. Madeleine's notions of
God and eternity were vague, like those of most
young people. She had been brought up in a
careful observance of the forms of the Episcopal
Church in Scotland, and she had always had a
certain devotional turn, which accompanies good
taste and purity of mind in young girls. But she
had never looked at life or death seriously, in the
true sense, at all. Sentimentally she had considered both, extensively of course; had she not
read all the poetry she could lay her hands on,
and a vast number of essays? Of late a voice
whose tones she had never before heard, still and
small, had spoken to her—spoken much and solemnly in her girlish heart, and had taught her,
in the silent suffering and doubt, the unseen
struggle she had undergone, great things. She
kept her own counsel; she listened, and was still;
and the chain of earth fell from her fair soul while
yet it held her fair form in its coil a little longer.

Madeleine had looked into her life to find the meaning of her Creator in it. She had found it, and she was ready for the summons, which was not to tarry long.

One day, when she had told Wilmot that she was wonderfully easy, had had quite a good night, and had hardly coughed at all since morning, he was sitting by her sofa, and she, lying with her face turned towards him, had fallen into a light sleep. He drew a coverlet closely round her, and signed to the nurse that she might leave the room. Then he sat quite still, his face rigid, his hands clasped, looking at her; looking at the thin pale face, with the blazing spots of red upon the cheek-bones, with the darkened eyelids, the sunken temples, the dry red lips, the damp, limp, golden hair. As in a phantasmagoria, the days at Kilsyth passed before him; the day of his arrival, the day the nurse had asked him whether the golden hair must be cut off, the day he had pronounced her out of danger. Outwardly calm and stern, what a storm of anguish he was tossed upon! Words and looks and little incidents—small things, but infinite to him—came up and tormented him. Then came a sense of unreality; it could not be, it was not the same Madeleine; this was not Kilsyth's beautiful daughter. His hands went up to his face, and a groan burst from his lips. The sound frightened him. He looked at her again; and as he looked, her eyes opened, and she began to speak. Then came the frightful, the inevitable cough. He lifted her upon his arm, kneeling by her side, and the paroxysm passed over. Then she looked at him very gently and sweetly, and said:

"Are we quite alone?"

"Yes."

"Do you remember one night at Kilsyth, when I was very ill, I asked you whether I was going to die?"

"I remember," he said, with a desperate effort to keep down a sob.

"And I told you I was very glad when you said, 'No.' Do you remember?"

"Yes—I remember."

She paused and looked at him; her blue eyes were as steady as they were bright. "If I asked

you, but I don't—I don't"—she put out her
wasted hand. He took the thin fingers in his,
and trembled at their touch—"because I know
—but if I did, you would not make me the same
answer now."

He did not speak, he did not look at her;
but her eyes pertinaciously sought his, and he
was forced to meet them. She smiled again, and
her fingers clasped themselves round his.

"You will always be papa's friend," she said.
"Poor papa—he will miss me very much; the
girls are too young as yet. And Ronald—I have
something to say to you about Ronald. Sit here,
close to me, in papa's chair, and listen."

He changed his seat in obedience to her, and
listened; his head bent down, and her golden
hair almost touching his shoulder.

"Something came between Ronald and me
for a little while," she said, her low voice, which
had hardly lost its sweetness at all, thrilling the
listener with inexpressible pain. "I cannot tell
what exactly; but it is all over now, and he is
—as he used to be—the best and kindest of

brothers. But there is someone—not papa; I am not talking of poor papa now—better and kinder still. Do you know whom I mean?" The sweet steady blue eyes looked at him quite innocent and unabashed. "I mean *you.*"

"Me!" he said, looking up hastily; "me!"

"Yes; best and kindest of all to me. And when Ronald will not have me any longer, I want you to promise me to be his friend too. They say he is hard in his disposition and his ways; he never was to me, but once for a little while; and I should like him to see you often, and be with you much, that he may be reminded of me. As long as he remembers me he will not be hard to anyone; and he will remember me whenever he sees you."

Thus the sister interpreted the brother's late repentance, and endeavoured to render it a source of blessing to the two men whom she loved.

"When you left Kilsyth," she said, "and came here, and when I heard the dreadful affliction that had befallen you, it made me very unhappy. It seemed, somehow, awful to me that sorrow should have come to you through me."

"It did not," he replied. "Don't think so; don't say so! Did anyone tell you so? It would have come all the same—"

"It would not," she said solemnly; "it would not. If I never felt it before, I must have come to feel it now, that I caused unconsciously a dreadful misfortune. You are here with me; you make suffering, you make death, light and easy to me. And you were away from *her* when she was dying who had a right to look for you by her side. I hope she has forgiven me where all is forgiven."

There was silence between them for a while. Wilmot's agony was quite beyond description, and almost beyond even his power of self-control. Madeleine was quite calm; but the bright red spots had faded away from her cheek-bones, and she was deadly pale. His eyes were fixed upon her face—eagerly, despairingly, as though he would have fixed it before them for ever, a white phantom to beset, of his free will, all his future life. Another racking fit of coughing came on, and then, when it had subsided, Madeleine fell again into one of the sudden short sleeps which had become habitual to her, and which told Wilmot so plainly of the progress of exhaustion. It was only of a few minutes' duration; and when she again awoke, her cheeks had the red spots on them once more. He watched her more and more eagerly, to see if she would resume the tone in which she had been speaking, and which, while it tortured him to listen to it, he had not the courage to interrupt or interdict. There was a little, a very little more excitement in the voice and in the eyes as she said,

"You are not going to be a doctor any more, they tell me, now that you are a rich man."

"No," he said, in a low but bitter tone. "I am done with doctoring. All my skill and knowledge have availed me nothing, and they are nothing to me any more."

"Nothing! And why?"

"O Madeleine," he said,—and as he spoke he

fell on his knees beside the sofa on which she lay—"how can you ask me? What have they done for me? They have not saved you. I asked nothing else—no other reward for all my years of labour and study and poverty and insignificance—nothing but this. Even at Kilsyth, when you had the fever, I asked nothing else. I got it then, for they did save you. Yes, thank God, they did save you then for a little time! But now, now—" And, forgetful of the agitation of his patient, forgetful of everything in this supreme agony, Chudleigh Wilmot hid his face in the coverlet of the sofa and wept— wept the burning and distracting tears it is so dreadful to see a man shed. Madeleine raised herself up, and tried to lift his head in her feeble, wasted hands. Then he recovered himself with a tremendous effort, and was calm.

"I must tell you," he said, "having said what you have heard. Madeleine, there is no sin, no shame in what I am going to tell you. I will tell it to your father and your brother yet; I would tell it to your husband, Madeleine. When

I went away from England, I took a vision with me. It was, that I might return some time and ask for your love. It faded, Madeleine; but I claim, as the one solitary consolation which life can ever bring me, to tell you this: you are the only woman I have ever loved."

Madeleine looked at him still; the colour rose higher and brighter on her wasted cheeks; the light blazed up in her blue eyes.

"Did you love me," she said, "because you saved my life?"

"I don't know, child. I loved you—I loved you! That is all I know. I know I ought not to say it now; but I must, I must!"

"Hush!" she said; "and don't shiver there, and don't cry. It is not for such as you to do either." He resumed his seat; she gave him her hand again, and lay still looking at him—looking at him with her blue eyes full of the inexplicably awful look which comes into the eyes of the dying. After a while she smiled.

"I am very glad you told me," she said. "People said you never cared for the patient, only for the *case;* but since you have been here I have known that was not true. It is better as it is. If your vision had come true, I must have died all the same, and then it would have been harder. It is easier now."

Another fit of coughing—a frightful paroxysm this time. Wilmot rang for the nurse, and Kilsyth and Lady Muriel entered the room with her.

* * * * *

Several hours later Madeleine was lying in the same place, still, tranquil, and at ease. She had had a long interval of respite from the cough, and was cheerful, even bright. Her father was there, and Ronald; Lady Muriel also, but sitting at some distance from her, and looking very sad.

When the time came at which Madeleine was to be removed to her bed, Ronald and Wilmot took leave; the first for the night, the second to return an hour later, and give final instructions to the nurse.

Wilmot's left hand hung down by his side as he stood near her, and Madeleine touched a ring upon his little finger.

"What is the motto on that ring?" she asked.

"The untranslateable French phrase, which I always think is like a shrug in words: *Quand même*," he replied.

The ring was the seal-ring which his wife had been used to wear. It struck him with a new and piercing pain, amid all the pains of this dreadful day, that Madeleine should have noticed it, and reminded him of it then.

"*Quand même*," she said softly. "Notwithstanding, even so—ah, it can't be said in English, but it means the same in every tongue." He bent over her, no one was near, her eyes met his; she said, "I am very happy—very happy, *quand même!*"

*   *   *   *   *

Wilmot went home and sat down to think—to think over the words he had spoken and heard. He was overpowered with the fatigue, the excitement, the emotion of the day. A thousand confused images floated before his weary eyes; the room seemed full of phantoms. Was this illness? Could it be possible? No, that must not be; he could not be ill; he had not time. After—yes, after, illness—anything! but not yet. He called for wine and bread, and ate and drank. His thoughts became clearer, and arranged themselves; then he became absorbed in reflection. He had told his servant he should require the carriage in an hour, and, hearing a noise in the hall, he started up, thinking the time had come. He opened his study-door, and called—

"Is that the brougham, Stephen?"

"No, sir," said the man, presenting himself with an air of having something important to say.

"What is it, then?" said Wilmot impatiently.

"A messenger from Brook-street, sir; Captain Kilsyth's man, sir."

Wilmot went out into the hall. The man was there, looking pale and frightened.

"What is it, Martin? what is it?"

"Captain Kilsyth sent me, sir, to let you know that Mrs. Caird is dead, sir,—a few minutes after you left, sir. Went off like a lamb. They didn't know it, sir, till the nurse came to lift her into bed."

CHAPTER IX.

FORLORN.

YES, she was dead; had died with a smile upon her lips; had died at peace and charity with all; had died knowing that the man whom she had looked up to and reverenced, had loved with all the pure and guileless love of her young heart, had loved her also, and had so loved her that he had suffered in silence, and only spoken when the confession could bring no remorse to her, even no longing regret for what might have been. Even no longing regret? No! " Happy, *quand même,*' were the last words that ever passed her lips; "happy, *quand même,*"—she had been something to him after all! In the few short and fleeting hours which she had passed between hearing Chudleigh Wilmot's confession, wrung from his heart by the great agony which possessed him, she had pondered over the words which he had spoken with inexpressible delight. What can we tell, we creatures moulded in coarser clay, creatures of baser passions, soiled in the perpetual contact with earth, its mean fears and gross aspirations, if aspirations they may be called,—what can we tell of the feelings of a young girl like this? Death, which we contemplate as the King of Terrors, threatening us with his uplifted dart, and destined to drag us away from the stage of life, bright with its tawdry tinsel and its garish splendour, came to her in softer and more kindly guise. For months she had been expecting the advent of the "shadow cloaked from head to foot," in whose gentle embrace she knew that she must shortly find herself. Those around her, her loving, doating father, Lady Muriel, Ronald, softened by the silent contemplation of her gradually-decreasing strength, the daily ebbing of physical force, the daily loosening of even the slight hold on life which she possessed, visible even to his unpractised eyes,—none of these had the smallest idea that the frail delicate creature, round whose couch they stood day by day

with forced smiles and feigned hope, knew better
than any of them, better even than he whose professional skill had never been brought into such
play, how swiftly the current of her life was bearing her on to the great rapids of Eternity. And if
before she had heard those burning words, inten-
sified by the agony shown in the choking voice
in which they found their utterance, she had
been able calmly and not unwillingly to contemplate her fate, how much greater had been her
resignation, how much more readily did she accept
the fiat when she learned that the one love of her
life had been returned; and that, despite of all
that had come between them, despite the interpo-
sition of the dread barrier which had apparently
so effectually separated them from each other, the
man who had been to her far beyond all others
had singled her out as the object of his adoration!

In those few last earthly hours the "what
might have been" had passed through her mind,
and passed away again, leaving behind it no trace
of anguish or remorse. Not only to Wilmot had
the time since their first acquaintance at Kilsyth

passed in review in phantasmagoric semblance; Madeleine had often gone through such scenes in the short drama, recollecting every detail, remembering much which had been overlooked even in his rapid summary. "What might have been!" Even suppose the dearest, the only real aspiration of her heart had been accomplished, and she had become Chudleigh Wilmot's wife, would not the inevitable end have had additional distress and misery to both of them? The inevitable end! for she must have died—she knew that; not for one instant did she imagine that any combination of circumstances different from what had actually occurred could have averted or postponed the fulfilment of the dread decree. Her married life had not been specially happy; then should she not have less regret in leaving it? Would not the pangs of parting be robbed of half their bitterness by the knowledge that her husband left behind would not sink under the blow? What might have been! Ah, Wilmot would feel her loss acutely, she knew that; the one outburst of grief, of passionate tenderness and heartfelt agony which had escaped him had told her that; but he would feel it less than if what might have been had been, and she had been taken away from him in the early days of their love and happiness.

A notion that such thoughts as these might have filled the mind of her for whom they mourned occurred to each of those by whom the dead girl was really loved, not indeed at once nor simultaneously, but at divers times, as they pondered over the blank which her loss had left in their lives. Among this number Mr. Ramsay Caird was not to be reckoned. The solemn announcement which, at his own request, Dr. Wilmot had made to him as to the impossibility of his wife's recovery and the probable short duration of her illness had had very little effect on the young man. What were the motives which prompted him were known to himself alone; but the *insouciance*, to use the mildest term for it, which had prompted him during the whole of his short married life seemed in no way diminished even by the dread news which had been communicated to him. He acknowledged that he had seen Dr. Wilmot, and had asked him his opinion; that that opinion had been very serious, and to some persons would have been alarming, but that he was not easily alarmed, and that he was utterly and entirely incredulous in the present instance. Madeleine had a bad cough, and was naturally delicate on her chest, and that sort of thing; she did not wrap up enough when she went out, and sat in draughts; but as to the way in which they all went on about her—well, they would find that he was right, and then they would be sorry they had listened to any such nonsense. He said this to Lady Muriel; for both Kilsyth and Ronald shrunk from any communication with him. Bitterest among all the bitter feelings which oppressed these two men, so different in mind and spirit, but with their love centred on the same object, was the thought that they had given up the guardianship of their treasure to one who was utterly unworthy of it, and, as one of them at least confessed to himself with keen remorse, had blighted two lives by unreasoning and shortsighted pride.

So, while his young wife had been gradually

declining, Ramsay Caird had made very little alteration in the mode of life which he had thought fit
to pursue since the earliest days of his marriage.
Relying principally on the fact, which he was
constantly urging, that he was of "no use," he
absented himself more and more from his home;
and when "doing duty" there, as he phrased it,
strove in no way to hide the dislike with which he
regarded the irksome task. Companionship was
necessary to Ramsay Caird, and was not to be
obtained, he found, among the class with whom
since his arrival in London and his domestication
in Brook-street he had been accustomed to as-
sociate. The men who had been pleasantly fa-
miliar with him in those days stood aloof, and
seemed by no means anxious to continue the acquaintance. They had come, soon after his marriage, and dined in the little red-flocked tank in
Squab-street, but that was principally for Madeleine's sake; and when rumours as to the newly-
founded *ménage* grew rife, and more especially
after Tommy Toshington's delightful story of seeing Caird at Madame Favorita's door had got

wind, the men generally agreed that he was a bad lot, and fought as shy of him as was compatible with common politeness. For it is to be noted that the loose-living Benedick, the married man who glories in his own escapades and talks with unctuous smack of his dissipations, is generally shunned by those men of his own set, who are by no means strait-laced, and forced to seek his company in a lower grade.

Ramsay Caird began to be bored and oppressed by his wife's illness, and by the constant presence of her father and brother at his house. It is true that he never saw these unwelcome visitors—on both sides any meeting was studiously avoided—but he could not help knowing of their being constantly with the invalid; and his own conscience, as much of it as he had ever possessed, did not fail to tell him what must be their indubitable opinion of him and his conduct. The companions too with whom he had taken up—for Ramsay Caird was essentially gregarious, and especially during the last few months had found the impossibility of living without excitement—the new companions with whom he consorted, and who were principally half-sporting, half-military, whole raffish adventurers, always well dressed, and retaining a certain hold on society, where they once had been well received,—these men encouraged Caird in his dislike to his home, and assisted him in the invention of plausible excuses to get away from it. The fact that he had "gone on to the turf," which he had at first taken every precaution to prevent his connections in Brook-street from becoming acquainted with, and which, when some kind common friend had told them of it, struck Kilsyth with silent horror, and aroused much burning and outspoken indignation in Ronald, was now put forward on every occasion, just as though it had been a legitimate business on which he was employed. "Meetings" were constantly taking place all over the country at which his attendance was indispensable, and he was soon well known as one of the regular frequenters of the betting-ring. On his return the servants in Squab-street could generally tell what had been the result of his betting speculations; but only to them and to one other person did he ever show his temper. And that one other person was Lady Muriel—the proud Lady Muriel—who in all matters between her husband and this man, who by her instrumentality had become the husband of her husband's daughter, had to be the go-between; to her it was left to soften his irregularities and gloss them over as best she might, and she alone possessed his confidence. To be the *confidante* of a gambler and the apologist for a debauchee was scarcely what Lady Muriel had expected when she gave her pledge to dying Stewart Caird, and when she intrigued and manœuvred so successfully in gaining her step-daughter's hand for Ramsay.

Three days before Madeleine's death Ramsay Caird announced to Lady Muriel, whom he stopped as she was about to ascend the stairs to the invalid's room, that he wanted to speak to her, and, on joining him in the red-flocked tank, told her that he was about to start that night for Paris. There were races at Chantilly in which he was very much interested, having a large sum at stake, and it was absolutely necessary that he should be

on the spot to watch and avail himself of the fluc-
tuations in the betting-ring. Then, for the first
time during their acquaintance, Lady Muriel
spoke out to her quondam protégé. The long-
repressed emotions under which she was suffering
seemed to have given her eloquence ; she drew a
vivid picture of "what might have been" if Ramsay's conduct had been different, and lashed his present life and pursuits, the company he kept, and the
general degradation into which he had fallen, with
an unsparing tongue. ,She implored him to give
up his intended journey, assuring him that he
either would not or could not understand the extreme danger of his wife's position, pointing out to
him what scandal must necessarily arise from his
absenting himself at such a time, and, telling him
that his past conduct during his married life, already sufficiently commented upon by the world,
might to a certain extent be condoned by his doing
his duty and devoting himself to his home for the
future. Ramsay listened impatiently, as men of
his stamp always listen to such advice, and then
he in his turn spoke out. He said that he would

be his own master, that he would brook no interference with his plans, that already he was a mere
cipher in his own house, which was invaded and
occupied by other people at their own pleasure,
and that he would stand it no longer; then, after
this outburst, he moderated his tone, apologised to
Lady Muriel for his violence, and told her that,
though the importance of his business arrangements and the largeness of his venture made it
absolutely necessary for him to go to Paris on this
occasion, yet it should be the last; he would do as
her ladyship wished him, as he felt he ought to do,
and his enemies should find that he was not so
black as by some persons he had been painted.

So Ramsay Caird and a select circle of Bri-
tish turfites took their departure by that night's
mail, and enjoyed themselves very much, smoking,
drinking, and playing cards whenever it was prac-
ticable on the journey. Most of them were men
whose acquaintance Caird had made some time
previously; but amongst them there was a French-
man, a M. Leroux, whom Ramsay had never previously seen, although the little gentleman said he

had frequently been in England, and seemed perfectly conversant with the English language, manners, and customs. He was a lively, vivacious, gasconading little fellow; and any temporary depression of spirits which Ramsay Caird may have felt after his interview with Lady Muriel quite vanished under the influence of M. Leroux's conversation. He and M. Leroux seemed to have taken a mutual liking to each other; they went together to the races, where Caird won a large sum of money, Leroux not being quite so fortunate; and on their return to Paris, Ramsay declined to join his English friends, and dined with Leroux and some very agreeable Frenchmen to whom Leroux had introduced him at the races. The dinner was excellent; and after they had done full justice to it, and to the wines which accompanied it, they all adjourned to some neighbouring rooms belonging to one of their number, where cards and dice were speedily introduced. Again Ramsay Caird's luck stood by him. *Malheureux en amour,* he was destined to be *heureux en jeu* on this occasion at least. Nothing could alter or diminish his flow of success; no matter what he played, lansquenet, baccarat, hazard, he won largely at them all; and when at a very late hour he left the rooms in company with Leroux and two of his friends, his pockets were filled with notes and gold. They were quite empty when they were examined about noon the next day by the attendants at the Morgue, whither Ramsay Caird's dead body, found in the Seine with a deep gash in its breast, had been conveyed.

M. Leroux and his friends did not come so well out of this little affair as they had expected. They knew that Ramsay was a stranger in Paris, known only to the English sporting-men in whose company he had arrived there, and who had probably returned to England. But they did not make allowance for the fact that of all cities Paris has a charm for the "English division," who, if they have won any money, linger for a few days amongst its pleasures, one of which undoubtedly is a frequent visit to the Morgue. By one of these late lingerers, no less a person than Captain Severn, the body of Ramsay Caird was seen and recognised; inquiries were at once set on foot; the waiter at the restaurant, the *concierge* at the house where the play had taken place, were examined, and gave their evidence. M. Leroux and his two friends were apprehended; one of the friends turned traitor (his share of the spoil had been too small), and Leroux and the other, being found guilty of murder under extenuating circumstances, were sentenced to the galleys for life.

The news of this catastrophe was conveyed to the Kilsyth family in a letter addressed by Captain Severn to Ronald, which letter lay unopened in Brook-street for several days. Ronald Kilsyth was far too much crushed and broken by the blow, which, for all their long expectation of its advent, had yet fallen suddenly upon them at the last, to attend to anything unconnected, as he imagined, with the dead. He had indeed carelessly glanced at the cover of this letter, with several others; but the handwriting was unfamiliar to him, and he put it aside, to be opened at a later opportunity. It was not until two or three days afterwards, when Ramsay Caird had been sought in vain, and

when Lady Muriel had confessed that he had confided to her his intention of going to Paris, that
Ronald recollected the letter in the strange handwriting with the Paris postmark. He sent for the
letter, and read it through without the smallest sign
of emotion. He was a hard man, Ronald Kilsyth,
and the softening effect of his sister's illness only
included her and those who were fond of her.
Ronald knew well enough that Ramsay Caird did
not come within this category, and he felt no pity
for his fate.

He communicated the news to his father more
as a matter of form than anything else; for the
shock of his beloved child's death had almost de-
prived Kilsyth of his reason. Like Rachel, he
refused to be comforted, and would sit hour after
hour in one position on his chair, his eyes fixed on
vacancy, his chin resting on his breast, his hands
idly clasped before him. Nothing seemed to rouse
him,—not even the news which had been conveyed
to Ronald in Captain Severn's letter. He comprehended it, for he said "Poor Ramsay!" once,
and once only; then heaved a deep sigh, and never

alluded to his dead son-in-law again. His thoughts were filled with reminiscences of his lost darling, and he had none to bestow on anyone else. "My poor Maddy!" "My bonnie lass!" "My own childie!"—he would sit and repeat these phrases over and over again; then steal away down to the house where all that was left of her still lay, and remain on his knees by the coffin, until Ronald would come and half forcibly lead him away. He left London immediately after the funeral, and never could be persuaded to return to it. After a while, the fresh mountain air, to which he had been so long accustomed, and away from which he was never well, had some of its old restorative effect, and Kilsyth recovered most of his physical strength and some of his old pleasure in field sports; but his zest for life was gone, and the gillies mourned the alteration in the chief whom they loved so much.

The death of Ramsay Caird under such horrible circumstances was a crushing blow to Lady Muriel. This, then, was the end of all her schemes and plots; this the result of so much mental agony and remorse endured by herself—of so much grief and cruel injustice inflicted by her on others. She had kept the promise she had made to Stewart Caird on his death-bed, two lives had been sacrificed, two loves had been blighted—but she had kept her promise. For the first time in her life "my lady's" courage failed her; and her conscience showed her how recklessly she had availed herself of the means to gain her ends. For the first time in her life she dreaded meeting the glances of the world. More than all men she dreaded Ronald Kilsyth, knowing as she did full well how she had used him for her own purposes, and with what lamentable results. She had been seriously affected by Madeleine's death—like many worldly people, never knowing how much she had loved the girl until she lost her; and now the fact of Ramsay's murder under such discreditable circumstances—a story which had been made public in the newspapers, where the world could glean the undeniable truth that the murdered man had left what was actually his wife's death-bed to attend some races—seemed to overwhelm her. The young

men who visited at the house had been in the
habit of expressing to each other great admiration
of Lady Muriel's "pluck"—that quality did not
desert her even at her worst. She made head
against her troubles, and never gave in ; but those
intimate enemies who saw her before she left London with her husband declared Lady Muriel to be
" quite broken" and a " thorough wreck."

And Chudleigh Wilmot? He lived, of course;
lived, and ate and drank, and pursued very much
his usual course of life. Well, no; not quite his
usual course of life. The effect of the death
of the one woman whom in his lifetime he had
loved was to him much as are the gunshot
wounds of which we sometimes hear officers and
army surgeons tell; wounds where the hit man
feels a slight concussion at the moment, and does
not know until a short time afterwards that he is
stunned, paralysed for ever. While Wilmot had
been watching the insidious progress of Madeleine's disease, his mental misery at times was most
acute; every variation in her was apparent to his
practised eye; and day by day he saw the de-

stroyer creeping stealthily onward in his attack,
without the smallest power to resist him. When
the bitter tidings of her death were brought by
Ronald's servant, the words fell upon Chudleigh
Wilmot's ear and smote him as if a sharp cut
from a whip had fallen upon him. She whom he
had loved so devotedly, so hopelessly, so selflessly,
was dead—he realised that. He knew that he
should never see the light in her blue eyes, never
hear the sweet soft tones of her voice again. He
was thankful that, under the impulse of his grief,
he had spoken to her out of his overcharged heart
and told her how he loved her. He dared not
have done it before, he dared not under any other
circumstances have confessed the passion for her
that had so long been the motive-power of his life;
but then—" Happy, *quand même !*" Her last words
—she never had spoken after that—her last words
were addressed to him, and told him of her happiness.

It was not until after the funeral that Wilmot
experienced the full effect of the blow, experienced
it in the dead dull blankness which seemed for the

second time to have fallen upon his life. He
had had something of the kind before, but nothing
equal in intensity to what he now suffered. He
felt as though the light had died out, and that
henceforward he was to walk in darkness, without
care, without hope, without interest in any mortal
thing. Previously he had found some relief in
hard study; now he found it impossible to fix his
attention on his books. The awful sense of something impending was perpetually upon him; the
more awful sense of something wanting in his life
never left him. The only time that a ray of comfort broke in upon him was when Ronald Kilsyth
would come and sit with him, and they would talk
of the dead girl for hours together, as Madeleine
had predicted they would do. They are very
much together now, these two men; Ronald has
risen in the service, and he and Wilmot are engaged in ameliorating the condition of the common
soldiers and their families. It was a work in which
Madeleine at one time took much interest; and
this was sufficient to recommend it to Wilmot,
who at once took it up.

He is a middle-aged man now, with a grizzled head and a worn grave face. He has wealth and fame, and might have any position; but the world can offer him nothing that arouses in him the slightest interest, unless it be associated with the memory of his lost love.

THE END.

LONDON:

ROBSON AND SON, GREAT NORTHERN PRINTING WORKS,
PANCRAS ROAD, N.W.